ELEMENT

A. L. Barker left school when she was sixteen and, after the Second World War, joined the BBC. Her debut collection of short stories, *Innocents*, won the first-ever Somerset Maugham Award in 1947, and her novel, *John Brown's Body*, was shortlisted for the Booker Prize in 1969. She is the author of ten novels, most recently *Zeph*, and eight short story collections.

BY THE SAME AUTHOR

Novels

Apology for a Hero
A Case Examined
The Middling
John Brown's Body
A Source of Embarrassment
A Heavy Feather
Relative Successes
The Gooseboy
The Woman Who Talked to Herself
The A. L. Barker Omnibus
Zeph

Stories

Innocents
Novelette
The Joy Ride and After
Lost upon the Roundabouts
Femina Real
Life Stories
No Word of Love
Any Excuse for a Party

A. L. Barker

ELEMENT OF DOUBT

Ghost Stories

VINTAGE

VINTAGE
20 Vauxhall Bridge Road, London SW1V 2SA

London Melbourne Sydney Auckland
Johannesburg and agencies throughout
the world

First published by Vintage, 1992

1 3 5 7 9 10 8 6 4 2

'Romney' from *Novelette* was originally published by Hogarth
Press, 1951

'Lost Journey' from *Haunted Travellers* was originally published by William Kimber, 1985

'Just In Time' from *After Midnight Stories* was originally published by William Kimber, 1985

'Element of Doubt' from *The Third Book of After Midnight
Stories* was originally published by William Kimber, 1987

'The Parrot' from *New Stories 2* was originally published by
The Arts Council, 1977

'Fetched' from *The Fifth Book of After Midnight Stories* was
originally published by William Kimber, 1991

'I'll Never Know' was originally published in *Winter's Tales*
new series 7, Constable, 1991

The following stories were commissioned by BBC Radio 4:
'The Paradise Garden', 'The Dress', 'The Game', 'You Have
to Laugh'

Phototypeset by Intype, London
Printed and bound in Great Britain by
Cox & Wyman Ltd, Reading, Berkshire

ISBN 0 09 919051 6

CONTENTS

Romney   1
Lost Journey   50
Just In Time   65
Element of Doubt   77
The Parrot   91
The Doll   100
Fur   107
The Paradise Garden   119
Fetched   126
The Dress   138
The Game   145
You Have to Laugh   153
I'll Never Know   160

ROMNEY

JOE RIGBY, AS usual, had started to gather up his luggage a little too late. The parcel of boots threatened to burst open and he was so occupied with it, with his canvas holdall and his raincoat, that his stick had to be tossed out to him as the train moved off. It landed clattering on the platform and somehow by then it was no longer the helpful gesture of his fellow-travellers. He picked it up as sadly as if he had been thrown out neck and crop.

On the journey down he had been sizing himself up. It had put him in one of his useless moods. When he surrendered his ticket he felt a pang because there was no return half. What a coward. He had a hotel room at the back of Charing Cross to be homesick for, this was his usual hankering after the known rather than the unknown.

The railway station was on a hill and he could look down into a rich haze, like pollen dust, settling over the village. Sounds of life floated to the top, a motor-bike bubbling, someone hammering, children bouncing a ball. Yet another strange place that was as personal to some people as the hollows in their beds. Somewhere beyond the spinach green woods was the place he was intended to know, though not so well, he thought, as the hollows in *his* bed.

The bus to Bessemer was waiting in the Market, a high old-fashioned yellow affair with a couple of sacks and a drum of paraffin on the roof. It was almost full already. Joe found a seat next to a little dry seed of a man and piled his luggage on the floor between them. His stick fell and hit his neighbour lightly on the knee.

1

'You weren't at the Board,' said the little man at once as if the contact had touched him off.

Joe drove his stick into the mound of luggage and it stood up between them like a small pole on a cairn. 'I've just come off the London train.'

'That's where we've all been, the Board.'

'Oh? What Board?'

'What Board?' The little man moved his hands as if he were throwing up pigeons. 'Why, the Board. *The* Board, you know.'

'Ah.'

His fellow-traveller looked reproving. 'It meets every three months and I've never missed in twenty years.'

'That's quite a record.'

The bus began to shake diligently. As it lumbered out of the Market Joe's neighbour peered wistfully into Joe's face and touched him like an anxious child. 'It suddenly came to me that I'd never so much as opened my mouth – except for "Yes" and "No" and "Hear-hear" – all the time I'd been going.'

'Why,' said Joe encouragingly, 'I should think that's another record.'

'But it doesn't do, it doesn't do at all. People think you're indifferent. In public affairs there's nothing worse than indifference. It weighed on me.' Joe could see how those bottle shoulders had drooped. 'Day after day. And at night I used to wake up with it on my chest. You see I knew I ought to put in a word. What word and when was what worried me. You won't credit it,' he said with pride, 'but it went on for best part of a year. Then this afternoon, this very afternoon, I spoke up. In front of them all and in the proper course of debate.'

'Bravo! What did you say?'

'I said, "Better be safe than sorry". They'd been arguing, you see, and it put the whole thing in a nutshell. They could see then that I was on my toes.' He pushed out his gentle jaw. 'I'm a man of action, public speaking doesn't come easy to me. But once in a while a man must get the better of his

2

weaknesses. Not for the glory of it, for the sake of his self-respect.' He locked his arms over his narrow chest with dignity.

Joe looked at him rather bleakly. God help him, he would have been grateful for a teaspoonful of that warming self-esteem. It's the other thing men live by, thought Joe. That and bread. And after the first stab it dies so quickly. You hardly know it's gone until someone tells you you're small beer and you can't deny it to yourself.

Of course Manning had been nice about it. 'You're the sort of fellow for this job. You're bedrock, Joe, and that's what youngsters need nowadays more than ever they did. There are too many bright sparks burning themselves out; we don't want them in the teaching profession. We want — you'll forgive me, Joe, because you'll know what I mean — we want to get back to the old-fashioned virtues.'

Joe hadn't forgiven him. A man of thirty can't forgive the word 'old-fashioned', especially applied to his virtues.

Before the war Joe had been one of the bright sparks. He and his circle at college were about to set the world on fire when it took flame without them. Joe joined the army; within a month he had trodden on a nail. He spent three years in and out of hospital, lost his foot, almost lost his leg. It had damped him down. Irrevocably, it seemed. He was going to teach; later he would take a resident post in some school and that would be his life. He wasn't really dissatisfied, except when he had these wry days of knowing that he had done nothing worth while.

And never will now, he thought, imagining the conflagrations he might have started in art, science, commerce or politics.

'How far is it to Bessemer?'

His little neighbour unlocked both arms and wiped a hand round his harsh chin.

'It's as far as they go. When they get to the Bessemer crossroads there's a bit of green with a signpost where the bus turns off. There's nothing more that way, you see, bar the Priory.'

'It's the Priory I'm going to.'

To Joe's surprise, the little man sharpened up like a gimlet. 'Ah! Are they at it again, then?'

'At what?'

'Why, at their – ' he hesitated and finished oddly, ' – hoping. What are they on to now?'

'I'm afraid I don't know what you're talking about.'

'To send from London! That must be Mr. Steen's idea.' His excitement suddenly faded. 'No doubt he'll find out a great deal, poor soul, but will it profit him? Much better let it rest. Sometimes the only good about the past is that it's past.'

'I'm afraid – ' repeated Joe, but the bus stopped and his neighbour scrambled out over Joe's knees with a hurried 'Good-day'.

Joe looked blankly after him. He couldn't make head or tail of it. Gossip, he supposed, and the wrong end of the stick. But it made him wonder what he was going into. There was always something. His last job had shocked him consistently for the first few weeks until he got used to the family, the big unholy Irish family with a passion for trouble. Dropping into people's lives he used to think – leaning towards the adventure he had never known – must be a bit like parachuting into enemy territory. People weren't enemies but they were on their guard, they had their own language and their own policies and he had to live precariously on the outskirts.

He was about to drop in most uncertain territory. He knew next to nothing about Bessemer Priory. Manning had arranged it all, Manning had interviewed Mr. Steen – the Mr. Steen whose past was better past.

Will it be sinister, wondered Joe, or just scandalous?

When the bus put him down at the crossroads and rattled away, he stood with his belongings about him, turning his square mild face with deliberation this way and that. It was very quiet, the cold blue of evening established under the trees creeping and darkening as he watched. There was nothing much to see; the lane where the bus had come, another lane bisecting it where the bus had gone – both masked by a deep scrubby copse – and ahead of him the entrance to the Priory. The gates were open and a green pebble-cobble drive ran away from them into the dusk. Sighing, Joe gathered up his luggage and began to walk.

He was tired. Such thoughts as he now had slipped idly to and fro, taking him immeasurably far from the present and, for that matter, from the future or the past. He dreamed as he walked. He did not hear the bats cheeping nor the companionable scrape of his parcel rubbing on his thigh. When he had walked about half a mile he became aware that his foot ached. He stopped to rest it and at the same moment it occurred to him that Mr. Steen's drive was unnecessarily long. He looked up with a flash of anger. He saw the Priory.

By some oversight Joe Rigby had never been near one of the stately homes of England. To him they were a phrase in a comic song; he was unprepared. Bessemer Priory broke gently, piercingly on his weariness and fixed the moment for him – one of those private moments that never fade, are never later than yesterday.

In the dusk there was no division between grey lawns and grey walls. The earth put forth Bessemer as a part of itself, a rich hoar budding into stone, and, as the ragged pods of cloister walls showed, as prone to blight or winter as any plant. The finger arches of window and doorway were filled with swarming black or with stems of citric-yellow light. Ecclesiastical, austere, the Priory had a benighted air, as if the world had shrunken round it, leaving it more splendid, more solitary, more vulnerable.

Joe was a humble soul and his arrival was unassuming. It did not need to be made more so by the collapse of his parcel of boots on the very threshold. Even as he announced himself – 'I'm the new tutor,' – and stepped past a panelled iron door and a sibilant manservant, his two pairs of boots broke out of their paper and clattered on the stone floor with the sound of ten men. With a rustle of shock the manservant hurried to gather them up.

'Thank God,' thought Joe, 'there was no-one else to hear.'

But he was wrong. As he stumped after his guide up the stairs, the man, who was some way ahead, stopped and called into the darkness: 'Now what are you doing there?' and a child's voice said: 'They've come for me, haven't they, Wick?'

'Nobody's come for you yet. Get back to bed and maybe they never will.'

Joe distinctly heard a sigh, not the full gusty sigh of a child, but the faint sorrowful breath of someone unutterably tired, unutterably hopeless. The manservant, reaching the first landing, switched on the light and revealed an empty corridor.

'Who was that?' asked Joe.

'Only the child.'

'*Only* the child? No-one else?'

'Oh, no-one else. The child — and his bad dreams.' Wick smiled as he ushered Joe towards another flight of stairs.

There was a fire in Joe's room, a gas-fire installed in what must have been a mighty hearth, now partially bricked up. Joe was sorry to see it. Logs, he would have thought, and — forgetting this was a bedroom — a roasting spit would be more in keeping. However, the rest of the room was up to expectation. There was a black Italian fourposter carved with ample nymphs and puffed-up cherubs, there were brocaded chairs and a pear-wood escritoire, an oak linen-fold clothes-press and a round stool with gros-point embroidery worn to shreds by someone's feet. An arched alcove, richly worked in stone to house a private altar, now held a washhand stand and a china ewer and basin painted with leviathan blue roses.

Wick set down the boots neatly pair by pair and placed Joe's holdall on a chair. Polite but discriminating, he bent to unpack it.

'No, leave it, please,' said Joe. 'I'll see to it.'

'Dinner is over, of course,' said Wick, straightening, 'but I have instructions to serve yours in your room and to see that you have everything you require.' He reached out and shifted an ashtray a quarter of an inch on a side-table, implying that he foresaw he had time to be particular because here was one who would not require much. 'Mr. Steen would like to see you in the library to-morrow morning at eleven.'

6

'Thank you.' Joe sat down heavily on the edge of the bed. 'Was I expected to-night?'

'Mr. Steen, I believe, thought you would not arrive until to-morrow morning. Miss Barbary gave provisional instructions in case you should come this evening.'

'Miss Barbary is Mr. Steen's daughter, I suppose?'

'His step-sister.' Wick rustled like a leaf. 'Mr. Steen has – one son only. I will attend to your dinner at once.'

'Wick – it is Wick, isn't it?'

'Sir?'

'Who was the child?'

'The child?'

'On the landing.'

'That was Master Harry.' Wick slipped out, smiling.

Joe took off one shoe and went with it to the window. He drew the curtains aside.

There was a thin rind of moon above the trees. Lawns, park and fumy woods were lamp-black now and smeared in with an impartial thumb. The density of the sky was only slightly less, still for the moment adulterated with the last of the light. Soon there would be nothing to choose between earth and heaven.

Master Harry and his bad dreams. Who did he think was coming for him?

Bessemer Priory, by the craftsmanship and the fair measure of godliness which had gone into its building, by bitter histories that had fired and sweetened it, was well equipped to humble the proud and still the turbulent. Joe was neither, yet he could not fail to be influenced. Taken down another peg or two, he was perilously modest; his natural gentleness became a waking dream. He peopled the place with so much of its ecclesiastical past that the sight of a housemaid or even of Wick during his first tentative explorations would have shocked him inexpressibly.

But he saw no-one. At nine o'clock in the morning only sparrows whittling in the ivy broached the stillness at Bessemer. Joe had breakfasted in his room as, apparently,

7

was the Continental custom of the elder Steens. When he came downstairs to where the boy had waited last night he saw how out of place a child would be.

The light, coming in here through a stained window, was left with nothing of sun or morning in it; they were thick splendid church colours, lozenges of blue and green and blood scarlet. This lower corridor was like a nave. From the capital of each arched doorway leaned out a homely or angelic face.

Joe wondered where the boy was. There was nothing to trace him by, or to hint at his existence. But then the Priory was not a child's house.

He went down into the hall. Himself and the dust – creeping soundlessly, dazzlingly in a shaft of sunlight – were the only things that moved there. He compared this entrenched serenity with the riotous mornings of his Irish family; *their* sound and fury began before one sun-up and hardly ended by the next one. Stone, he thought, was more likely to enter into you than iron. Who wouldn't try for a shell as hard and beautiful as this? He let his eyes travel to the very limits of it. In the vaulted roof, at the intersections of the ribs, the bosses were cut into brittle flowers. And it was at that moment that he thought of the great fallibility of the shell, the hollowness which the enemy can inhabit as well as the friend.

Last night, and again this morning, he had an odd impression that there might be an enemy here. It was quite impersonal, as if something had been imposed on this place which should have been open to nothing but its own dissolution. For no reason except that he owned the Priory, Joe was inclined to blame Mr. Steen. When they met he saw at once how wrong he was.

Steen was no enemy. A more unharmful man it would be impossible to find. His innocuousness was negative since it came from neither kindness nor simplicity, but from indifference. Obviously he gave to affairs and events an adequate attention – no more. He received Joe courteously, looked him over with the dispassion of a man concerned more for

the possible habits of a newcomer to his table than the capa-
bilities of one who was to have sole charge of his son's
formative years.

'I hope you are comfortable in your room?' He waited
politely for Joe's assurance. Having received it and satisfied
himself that Joe, though rugged, was not likely to be crude,
he sat back in his chair as if the interview had already served
its purpose.

'I suppose Dr. Manning told you all about me?' ventured
Joe.

'Indeed, yes. I was quite satisfied. Your function will be to
prepare the child for his first public school. How long that
will take I have no idea, but naturally I wish it to be
accomplished as quickly as possible. You will find his edu-
cation has been neglected. He can read and write – little else.
He is, I believe,' said Mr. Steen without mockery, 'rather
slow.'

Joe felt a certain sympathy for the boy. One or two people
referred to Joe Rigby as 'rather slow'. He asked, 'How old
is your son?'

Quite an extraordinary change came over Mr. Steen. His
smooth cheeks grew grey, his whole face softened dreadfully,
those bleak incurious eyes of his filled with the most abject
pain and despair.

Joe was appalled. At first he thought Steen had had some
kind of seizure. Then he realised it was no physical anguish.
This man's indifference was rigorously put on as a blind and
an antidote. He used it against the suffering of his mind.

Joe did not know what to do. If his perfectly ordinary
question had brought Steen to this pass, in God's name what
could be wrong with the boy? Fresh in his memory was the
sound of that thin voice, 'They've come for me, haven't they,
Wick?' and the sigh that followed.

But if there was something – anything – why hadn't Manning said? It wasn't like Manning to be uninformed. And
what could be wrong, unless the child were mad or monstrous?

Mr. Steen stood up. 'I'll send for the child,' he said calmly.

All that remained of his violence was the greyness in his cheek. He pulled at the tasselled bellrope by the hearth and as an after-thought answered Joe's question. 'He is eight years old.'

But nothing was explained when the boy came. Harry Steen was no monster, and if he was mad, then this was one of his lucid periods. He came in quietly, a thin small child, not handsome, not ugly. Brown hair sprouted over his eyes, his soft collar was too big for his narrow neck. He was very like his father – the same bird's beak of a nose and the same curiously fresh pallor. He had pulled his socks up strenuously round his knees, uncovering black elastic garters.

He came slowly forward in his creaking shoes. Their noise shamed him and Joe felt his relief when he reached the desk where his father sat.

Steen got up without looking at him. 'I leave him to you,' he said to Joe. 'Order what books you need and let me have the bills. I should like a report on his progress in two months' time.'

He was gone before Joe could frame any of the questions he wanted to ask. The boy stood with bowed head. He seemed to be dwelling on the subject of his noisy shoes.

'Well, Harry, did they tell you about me?'

'I knew you were coming.'

'And what I was coming for?'

'Oh yes.' He looked up and Joe saw that he had blue eyes of surprising warmth and cloudiness. 'I'm sorry.'

'Sorry? Don't you want to learn?'

'I should like to, very much,' he said in his precise way. 'But what I'm sorry about is you having a lost journey. Because I don't expect to be here very long.'

Joe sat himself on a corner of Mr. Steen's desk. 'I'd like to get this clear, Harry. Your father didn't say anything about your going away.'

'He doesn't know.'

'I see. And when are you thinking of going?'

'Soon.' With the ghost of that sigh Joe had heard before, he returned to the contemplation of his shoes.

'When they come for you, I suppose?' hazarded Joe. Shocked and at sea, the boy flung up his head. 'I only know you're expecting someone because you said so yourself last night. Remember?' Looking into those wide opaque eyes, Joe foresaw that never from them would he know what went on. They would darken perhaps as they had now, with fright, but if he had not known there was cause for fear – in Harry's mind at least – they might as easily be dark with anger, or sorrow, or longing, or even a sombre happiness. 'You remember what you said? You heard me come in and thought I was – who is it you're expecting, Harry?'

The child had his dignity. He drew up, drew apart, with a sense of fitness no less real because it was forlorn.

'I think you must have been mistaken. I'm not expecting anyone.'

Miss Barbary Steen, whom Joe met at lunch, was a tiny flowerlike lady, not so much old as requiring to be thought so. Over her fair hair, just beginning to be faded, she wore a lace cap. Her black dress, the white fichu, the cameo brooch, were the crisp decent uniform of age. But her cheeks were still pink, her eyes bright, and not one blue vein stood up on her plump hands.

She liked to talk, seemed in fact designed for it and was unfeignedly glad at Joe's coming. And so, for the first time, was Joe, partly because he could imagine how one-sided conversations with her step-brother must be and because he always wished people well; partly because be could not expect to get anywhere with Mr. Steen and did not know how far he would progress with Harry. It seemed to Joe as Miss Barbary made her pleasure apparent that at least he would be able to serve one member of the family – simply by being there for her to talk to.

She did undoubtedly run on, in a sweet imponderable way which Joe found attractive. When Mr. Steen spoke he managed to do so without becoming the least embroiled in the conversation, and made no attempt to amend some of Miss Barbary's fanciful statements. Urbane, unencumbered

11

almost to the point of slipperiness, it was hard to believe there could be in him so much as a pocket of violence. Yet there it was, not a pocket but a gulf.

Miss Barbary, Joe thought, was aware of it, aware too of its source. Indeed, her skating over her stepbrother's fine ice was probably her way of understanding. It was there between them, whatever it was. A family affair, concluded Joe, and none of his, except in so far as it affected Harry.

'I hope,' Miss Barbary sparkled at him across her soup, 'you're not the kind of person who likes to be involved.'

'Involved?' Joe was afraid she had read his thoughts.

'I mean in affairs, arts and sciences, progress, you know. Or politics. So many people feel they must. I'm sure it's an excellent thing, but here one can't, except by correspondence. Or there's the phone. But the village is two miles away and even there I'm afraid they're not alive to the rest of the world. You might start something, of course – '

'I never was very publicly-minded,' said Joe.

'Hunting, yes,' went on Miss Barbary as if he had asked a question. 'But the horses are gone. You would have to hire something from the village and I don't know what you would get. Here at the Priory we used to keep some of the best hunters in the country. They were magnificent.' Her pride failed her all at once and she cried sadly, 'Poor things!'

'Poor? They must have been anything but that,' said Joe, smiling.

'Oh, at the end they were – ' To his surprise she broke off in confusion, passed him the bread which he did not want, and hurried on with – 'I always think animals are poor – it's their being dumb – even lions – I meant that the horses were poor because they couldn't speak – '

'My sister means she was sorry for the horses when I had them shot,' said Mr. Steen calmly. 'Will you ring for the next course, Barbary?'

This had a quenching effect. Miss Barbary looked at Joe, obviously expecting him to share her horror. As obviously realising that he couldn't, she bravely launched herself again and skimmed from topic to topic without coming to grief and without – as Joe observed – once mentioning Harry.

When the coffee arrived Mr. Steen left them to attend to some business with his bailiff. Miss Barbary made Joe bring his coffee over to a chair by the window. She began to give him a history of the gardens.

'Miss Steen,' Joe said cautiously in the first pause that offered, 'I'd like a word with you about Harry.' Gingerly he set down his shell of a coffee-cup, prepared, as he felt he had better be, for any possible reaction. 'I met him just this morning. Is there anything you could tell me about him, to help in getting to know him?'

'Harry?' Her voice had the reluctance of someone asked to turn to a dull subject. 'I don't think there's anything to tell you about Harry. You won't find him difficult to know. No particular vices or virtues. He can be very dull at times, which is tiresome, and his handkerchiefs are always filthy.' Miss Barbary stirred her coffee briskly. 'Oh, Harry's just an ordinary small boy.'

Joe doubted it. Walking with Harry that afternoon he wondered how much Miss Barbary saw of the boy. His rough hair, his chicken neck, his draggled socks, his grimy handkerchiefs – but had she noticed that odd urgent forward poke of his head, at once hounded and defiant? Had she ever tried reading some meaning in those clouded eyes? It was time someone looked at Master Steen. Ordinary perhaps he was intended to be, ordinary perhaps he usually was, ordinary now he certainly was not.

'What do you do with yourself most afternoons?' Joe asked him.

'I walk about.'

'Not all the time?'

'Oh yes. I walk like mad.'

'Are you so fond of it?'

'It makes me sleep.'

'You find it hard to sleep?'

'Sometimes.'

13

Joe said, smiling, 'I'm obliged to count sheep, I could never make your pace.'

Harry kicked at a tussock of grass. 'You've got a bad foot, haven't you?'

'No, I've a very good foot. It's made of light-weight steel alloy. The only trouble is that the rest of me isn't steel alloy too.'

'I suppose your foot was – shot off?'

'No. I had a rusty nail in my shoe.'

Harry's interest died, but he was kind. 'There's a seat over there under that tree. If you'd like a rest, I'd wait.'

'Thank you. I'd appreciate it while I fill my pipe.'

Harry came with him and sat down, but scarcely had the seat of his trousers touched the wood when he was up and off. Joe watched him stalking aimlessly about, scuffing his feet, as insensible to the beauty of the marked and failing Priory, the shadows shuttling across the golden lawns, the great galleon elms, as a fly creeping on a painted window. It was saddening, Joe thought, that it should all have come down through its holy and secular glories to this, one small indifferent boy with his air of being no more than a bird of passage.

It was at that moment that something – and afterwards Joe quite uselessly pondered what – made him turn and look behind him at the tree. Someone had carved a name in the bark, high up; a single word cut in deep. 'Romney'.

Carving on the trunks of trees being common enough where there are boys or men, Joe would have found little to remark on had the name been Tom, Dick – or Harry. 'Romney' was surprising. It was a graceful name and to Joe evocative of something fine and spacious. He called Harry over and pointed it out to him. 'Anyone you know?'

Harry gave him a look hardly more than a flicker. He climbed on to the seat, reached up and felt each letter with his fingertips. 'He said it would grow with the tree.'

'Who did, Harry?'

The boy was suddenly immensely interested in the tree itself. 'I've climbed this, you know. Right to the top. I suppose

14

it's a mile high. There's an owl lives here, he dropped a dead mouse on me once and I put it on the seat for him. He's a tawny owl, I think. Don't owls ever come out in the day?'

'No,' said Joe, 'not if they can avoid it. Harry – '

'Come on!' cried Harry desperately, 'I'll race you to the gate – ' His assumption of boisterousness failed him, he broke off scarlet-faced looking at Joe's foot.

'Harry, who is "Romney"?'

'No-one.'

'He carves his name as if he were someone.'

'I tell you he isn't! He's no-one! He's nothing!' The dense blue eyes were fierce, fanatical. He snatched up a tuft of earth and thrust it at Joe. 'He's not even this – not now – he's been dead a year.' The grit of earth in his hand seemed to calm him. He looked down at it and said flatly, 'Dead people are no-one.'

Joe took the grass from him. 'Let's go on with our walk.'

As they crossed the park Joe talked to him about lessons. Harry nodded obediently but it was only a mark of respect. His thoughts and emotions took their own way and when Joe finished, he said, 'I'm sorry I didn't answer your question. It was rude of me. If you still want me to, I'll tell you.'

'I should like an answer,' said Joe, 'but not if it upsets you so much to give one.'

'I wasn't upset. What was it you wanted to know?'

Joe looked at him sharply. He saw by lips and chin that the child was schooling himself to this.

'I wondered who Romney was.'

'He was my brother.'

'I'm sorry, Harry.'

'You haven't asked what happened to him. He was shot in the woods.' Ahead of them was a flounce of green copse. 'In there.'

'Shot? Who by?'

Harry's face was unchildish, hard. 'They say he shot himself.'

*

It meant something to Joe, being able to fix the source of the undertow at the Priory. And how much – even from the beginning when he knew next to nothing about the other Steen boy – could be attributed to that source! The cryptic comments of the man in the bus; the father's too green memory and his pain at mention of the word 'son'; his indifference to the child who was left; Miss Barbary's tact; Harry's unchildishness; and surely it was this private tragedy which had been driven like a wedge into the earned impersonal peace of the Priory itself? Joe thought so. Knowing the harsh logic of children he also thought that Harry's expectation of being taken away had been roused by his brother's going. How overwhelmingly right he was in that he had yet to learn. For the present he was relieved at knowing – as he thought he did – of the way matters stood. For Harry's sake he ought to know more.

There was only one person to tell him. Miss Barbary's tact had been stretched to the utmost over lunch. What she knew about her stepbrother's family she was bound, sooner or later, to let fall. It happened the same evening because Miss Barbary burned to tell it to Joe. It was in fact the legitimate expression of *her* grief.

Joe came downstairs an hour before dinner to find himself a book from the library. Miss Barbary, in the hall, was bundling into a woollen cloak for her evening stroll.

'You shall come too, Mr. Rigby,' she said, 'and talk to me.'

Joe thought there was little risk of his carrying any great burden of conversation. He went in hopes of learning more about Romney.

'Well, how do you find Harry?' said Miss Barbary as they came out into the enormous evening shadow of the Priory. 'Poor child, he's so orthodox. But then one needn't pity him for that. The orthodox have the best chance of survival, haven't they, Mr Rigby?'

'I can't agree with you. Neither can I think Harry orthodox. I wish he were.'

'Had you been here a year ago you would know what I mean.'

'When Romney was alive?'

She looked at him with surprise and the jealousy of the dispossessed. 'What do you know about Romney?'

'Only that he was Harry's brother and that he died a year ago.'

'Harry's brother – is that all you know?' said Miss Barbary contemptuously. 'Why, it was a matter of incredulity, of positive unbelief, that two such sons could be born of the same parents.' Joe felt the trembling of her arm as he helped her down the terrace steps. 'Yes, he died. A few days after his seventeenth birthday he fell on his gun in those woods over there.'

She gathered her cloak about her against the evening air. 'I have illusions about death, Mr. Rigby. They are permissible at my age. At least I have no illusion as to what *you* would call them. In this last year I have seen a great deal of Romney. You think I mean his ghost, but there could never be a ghost for him, he was not one to take to half-measures.

'When you look at Bessemer you see the gardens, the park and the Priory and you know it is beautiful. When I look I see Romney. The more beautiful it is, the more moods it has, the more I see him. It was his setting. He was rather like a diamond, Mr. Rigby, and now that he has dropped out of his setting, this little pip of a Harry can never take his place.'

'Harry was fond of him, I suppose?'

'He worshipped him. But then, who didn't? Everyone loved Romney.'

'What was he like?'

'More beautiful than any man, woman or child I have ever seen. There are no portraits of him. When he died, my brother destroyed them himself. In the same way,' said Miss Barbary evenly, 'he shot the hunters Romney used to ride. He threw his guns into the furnace. He closed the entire wing where Romney's rooms were. He forbade his name to be mentioned. All this to help him forget. Forget! As if he should even try! Isn't such a memory to be treasured? Isn't God to be thanked for it? It's selfish, selfish madness to forget perfection because you've lost it.'

'From the little I know of Mr. Steen,' said Joe, 'he appears to be suffering from very great pain of mind. I don't think he has forgotten.'

'He can't expect to. He and Romney were such companions, they worked together on the estate, they hunted together, they travelled together, they were more like brothers than father and son. Those troublesome ages young people have – speechless and spotty, or callow and bumptious – they never came to Romney. He was always beautiful to look at and he had a wit any man would have envied. But with all that, he was a warm-hearted generous boy and he had a heart of gold. Mrs. Steen died when Harry was born and from then onwards Romney looked on me as his mother.' Miss Barbary turned her face away. 'Does my brother think his loss is greater than mine? I would as soon try to forget the spring of the year as forget Romney.'

'I'm glad you told me,' said Joe. 'I might so easily have upset you without meaning to.'

'Sometimes I feel I can't bear it. My brother is making hermits of us and I am not – I never was – a solitary person. Romney was like me. He loved company. So did his father then. The Priory was a very different place – houseparties, balls, meets, cricket-weeks – there were always friends, always,' cried poor Miss Barbary. 'Now no-one comes because no-one is allowed to, not even other members of the family.'

'In time,' said Joe comfortingly, though he could not help feeling that time was more likely to consolidate the split in Mr. Steen. 'So it must be the loss of his brother that is troubling Harry.'

Miss Barbary laughed. It was a light and pleasant laugh but it grated on Joe.

'If there is anything troubling Harry, it will be the need of a new popgun or simply fear that he may be expected to work now you've come. Harry is a normal healthy small boy and you should know that healthy small boys don't sustain

sorrow more than a day or two. Harry has practically forgotten his brother. That's as it should be. But you'll have to be
firm with him, he is inclined to sulk. Now I think we should
be going back, there's quite a mist coming in across the park.'

There was, a cold thin steam climbing out of the hollows.
By the time dinner was over and Joe had gone up to his room
the ground below the terrace was as full of stealthy motion
as a vat of simmering milk. He pulled his chair to the window
and sat watching the industry of it. As the moon rose, the
mist thickened, laid, and the Bessemer acres were ghosts of
themselves.

Half-measures, thought Joe. I suppose it was Romney *I*
could see. He must have been a prodigy indeed to make such
an impression. Beauty has to be strong, stronger than evil,
to persist after death in places where people have been.

True, the impression he received was not all goodness and
light. But how should there not be something violent about
it when the boy was so violently cut off? To the family at
the Priory it must have been like the end of the sun.

Someone knocked at Joe's door and when he called 'Come
in', a bunch of stubby fingers appeared discreetly on the edge.

'Can I have a word with you, sir?'

Joe got up and opened the door wide. 'Come in. It's Mrs.
Brewer, isn't it?'

'Brewer, sir. The "Mrs." part is dead and gone.' She shut
the door firmly behind her, a tall old woman in a homely
white apron. 'Thank you, sir, I'd sooner stand. I apologise
for intruding on you but what I've to say won't take long.'
Joe found himself being quite openly summed up by a pair
of direct, almost hard grey eyes. 'Did Miss Steen tell you that
I've had the charge of Master Harry?'

'She told me you were his nurse.'

'I've come to you because you're taking him now and
there's something you should know. No-one else will tell you
because no-one else knows of it.'

'What is it?'

'Lately Master Harry has been leaving his bed at nights

and walking about. How often, I don't know, but I've caught him at it three times.'

'Just walking about?'

'As far as I know.'

'Has he said why?'

'There was a time when I knew what was in Master Harry's mind and didn't need to ask. If there was anything I couldn't know, he told me. Now,' she said grimly, 'I need to ask but he doesn't need to tell.'

'Didn't you speak to Mr. Steen or Miss Steen about this?'

'It's been on my mind, indeed, but I was afraid to.'

'Afraid? They would be more inclined to blame you for not telling them.'

'It's the boy I'm afraid for. They would say I must lock him in his room at nights.'

'You think that would be a bad thing?'

She said bluntly, 'Do you think it would be a good thing?'

'There's something the matter with the child. Have you any idea what it is?'

'The matter is that he cannot be a child.'

'Since when?'

'I can't put a term to it.'

'Would you say — since his brother died?'

Old Mrs. Brewer's mouth shut so hard that Joe thought she was not going to answer. Indeed it took her a full moment to relax enough to say, 'Perhaps.'

'Mightn't he be fretting?'

'I don't know if I can make myself clear,' she said painfully. 'You're a stranger, sir, and it's unseemly that I should come to you behind Mr. Steen's and Miss Barbary's backs. But I come for the child's sake. It's more than time he was stopped. I've tried and tried but he's beyond me.'

'What must he be stopped at?'

She touched her white apron here and there, taking comfort from the fact that it at least still knew and kept its place. 'It isn't so much him as what's riding him. A twig of a child to be stretched to breaking-point!'

'But you've no idea what's troubling him?'

'I wouldn't be here if I had, sir. I wouldn't be here if Mr. Steen and Miss Barbary – ' she floundered, coloured, ' – if they hadn't a blind spot for Master Harry.'

'They think you're fussing, I suppose. Well, as you say, I'm a stranger, but that means I get an outsider's view and if ever I saw a child with a load on his mind, that child is Harry. Were you a nurse to the other boy, too?'

'I came here with Mrs. Steen when she was married.'

'And what did you think of Romney?'

'I'm not at liberty to say, sir.'

'Why not?'

'Mr. Romney is dead.'

'I know that,' Joe said impatiently. 'I'm not asking you to tell me family secrets or speak ill of him. I wanted your personal opinion.'

'One can only speak as one finds, sir.' Those grey eyes were undeniably hard now. They left Joe in no doubt as to what Mrs. Brewer had found. 'Will you excuse me? I have to prepare Miss Barbary's tray.'

When she had gone Joe drew the curtains over the window and the flocculent mist. A matter of 'de mortuis nil nisi bonum', and one who did not love the beloved. Romney's fault, or Mrs. Brewer's? Hers, more likely. She had the Puritan touch and by all accounts the boy had not. He could have been shallow and feckless to her and she a deposed childhood dragon to him.

She did care, though, for Harry. She cared a great deal and she was worried or she would never have brought herself to interfere in the affairs of the family; to interfere, moreover, through the medium of an outsider. To the old-fashioned servant that was a crime of presumption.

Joe took up his pipe, began to fill it, then laid it down. On impulse he left his room and went along the corridor.

The last door on the left was Harry's. He had fixed a transfer picture on the upper panel. It had been there some time because it was half rubbed off. Joe peered at it and made out what appeared to be the grey shape of some kind of rat.

He touched the handle very gently, hesitated, then turned it and pushed the door ajar.

Harry was not in bed. He was sitting bolt upright in a huge wooden chair, sketchy as a puppet in his blue and white pyjamas. There was a night-light burning on a side-table; it cast dark hollows along the bones of Harry's small undistinguished skull and until Joe went close he could not see his eyes nor the whiteness of his fingers gripping the arms of the chair.

'Why, Harry – '

The child did not move. Stooping, Joe looked into his face and was disconcerted to find those clouded blue eyes gazing steadily into his.

'Why are you sitting here like this?'

The sticklike bones under the pyjama jacket braced themselves even more sternly. 'Do I look frightened?'

'Of course not. Who said you did?'

'It mustn't be said.' Harry relaxed and lay back in the chair. 'That's the only thing I'm frightened of – people saying I'm frightened.'

'Who isn't? It makes heroes of some of us. Whether you're going to be a hero or not depends on what you're frightened of.'

'Does it?'

'If it's fire or water or heights, you have to cut quite a dash proving you're not scared. If it's something not so spectacular the chances are no-one will know you were frightened or that you overcame your fright. What matters in the long run, of course, is not the other people but how you seem to yourself.'

'Oh, no,' said Harry, 'not to me it isn't. To me I shall seem frightened, I shall *be* frightened, but I can bear that so long as no-one else sees it.' He added, by way of information, 'It's not fire or water or heights.'

'I see. Well you'd better go back to bed now.'

Harry moved obediently. As he lay down and Joe drew the covers over him his body was relaxed but the uncandid eyes were watchful. He was doubled and ready inside for the questions he expected.

'A bold front seems everything, doesn't it?' said Joe. 'It's later on that you'll find other people's opinions of you, however good, won't give you peace if your opinion of yourself is poor.'

Whether Harry understood, he did not know. The boy lay there gazing steadily and once again Joe was struck by the warmth in his eyes. A child with strong natural affection. On whom, thought Joe pityingly, was he able to spend that? No longer on his brother Romney; there was only old Mrs. Brewer. If anyone else cared, they had not let it be seen and at Harry's age one could not deduce love, or presume it.

Joe sat down on the bed beside him. 'Can you see, Harry, how believing well of yourself can keep you up to scratch? You have to try all the time to live up to it. Of course you can't succeed all the time, but most people have something they remember, something they once did, which brought them flush with their golden opinions of themselves. It's a good thing to have, however small and trivial it may seem to other people.'

Harry pushed himself up on one elbow. 'What have you got?'

'I?'

'To remember.'

Joe smiled. 'Nothing.'

Harry did not smile back. 'You were in the war, weren't you? Did you ever kill a German?'

'I wasn't ever called upon to do that. And if I had been, I doubt I'm of stern enough stuff to try living up to it.'

Harry lay back on his pillow. His eyes were suddenly blank and cold; it was as if he were looking not at Joe, but at immeasurable wastes between them.

'Try to sleep now.' Joe pushed back the hair on the child's forehead. It troubled him to find the skin hot and damp under his fingers. 'Do you mind if I sit in this chair awhile?'

Harry came back from his distances, his face sharpening with suspicion. 'Why?'

'Not of course if you don't care about it – I was feeling a bit lonely and in need of company.'

'Is that why you came?'

'Of course.'

Harry smiled – it was the first time Joe had seen him do so. 'I shan't be company if I go to sleep.'

'Your snores will be more companionable than the ticking of my clock.' Joe settled himself in the chair and as Harry was still eyeing him doubtfully, asked chattily, 'What's that a picture of, outside on your door?'

'A rat.'

'Brother rat?'

'That's what Romney called me. He put it there.'

He was lying tranquilly enough, his hands by his narrow sides.

'You miss your brother, don't you, Harry?'

'I would give everything I have, everything in the world – I would give the world – to get him back.'

'I knew,' Joe said gently, 'that you loved Romney very much.'

Harry turned over, gripping his pillow with both hands. 'I hated him.'

If ever a man was at a loss, Joe Rigby was. He had not expected a problem in Harry Steen and obviously no-one else, with the exception of old Mrs. Brewer, believed that he had a problem. What they saw in Harry was a dullish aimless small boy, draggled after the manner of his kind but amenable and easy enough to handle. What Joe saw was a lonely ardent child with something far from childish on his mind. Until it was removed there could be no headway, no response to all Joe's efforts. It was as unrewarding and as unwise as harping on an overtaut string. How to relieve Harry of his burden, how even to discover the nature of the burden, with only opposition from Harry and unawareness from everyone else, was a task that dismayed the unenquiring Joe. He had never ferreted. His respect for other people's privacy was too profound.

This he could say with certainty – whatever it was that oppressed Harry, that had broken Mr. Steen and invoked a comfortless sense of anguish and violence in the peace of the Priory, was the death of Romney. What Romney had been that his death should inflict so much, Joe was free to imagine. He had Miss Barbary's eulogies, old Mrs. Brewer's laconicism and Harry's hatred to go by. Mr. Steen's silence was hardly a pointer, it confirmed the grief of a man who had loved his son whatever at heart that son had been.

Joe was troubled to find that Harry's warmth was the warmth of hate rather than of love. It would have been out of place in any child, but Harry's hatred of the dead was a perversion.

During the next few days Joe ordered and received school-books and equipment. He sounded the depths of Harry's practical knowledge and found them shallow. On the other hand he had a curiously deep understanding; one would have said he was more ready to face life than many boys twice his age, were it not for that something in him which Joe could only describe as 'off balance.'

There was, too, an unspoken conviction that his time was limited. Joe had to contend with that. Harry came to his lessons with the resigned politeness of one who knows it is no use, and when interest carried him away it left him as unhappy and angry as if he had been tricked.

'I wish you'd come before,' he said one day.

'Before what?'

'Before.' Lovingly, hopelessly, he stored his new books away in his new desk.

If he was to get anywhere with Harry, thought Joe, he must use that unsteadiness, that 'off balance' to overthrow the boy momentarily and shock his secret out of him. Joe believed he saw how it might be done.

Old Mrs. Brewer, sorting linen in the housekeeper's room, had a visit from the new tutor.

'You're the only one who *would* help me,' he said. 'The question is, can you?'

She no longer needed to size Joe up but she watched him

faithfully, not so much to analyse his thoughts as to keep abreast of them.

'I'm quite sure,' went on Joe, 'that whatever is troubling Harry is bound up with his brother. It's not a thing he's going to confide in me or anyone else. He'll keep it to himself until he cracks. God knows when that will be. For his sake we can't afford to wait. While he has this on his mind I can do very little with him. I'm wasting my time. I'm going to try getting him to give himself away.' He looked steadily into the old woman's eyes and she into his. 'For that I want something of Romney's, something that was very much his and known to be his. Something he used every day. Is there such a thing left? And if there is, how can I borrow it?'

Mrs. Brewer turned away. She shook out a guest towel, spread it on the table and went over it with her finger tips. She looked into it here and there before she folded it back into its squares. Her finger stayed on the blue embroidered 'S' in the corner.

'Perhaps,' she said.

'I want it now,' said Joe.

Mrs. Brewer looked at him from under her brows and made a decision. Once she had made it she was past surprise. She said to herself, 'What I do, I do for the boy,' and left it at that for the present. She alone knew she was not past recrimination – *that* she would inflict on herself time and again.

'His rooms are all shut up,' she said to Joe, 'and locked. Mr. Steen has the keys but I have another set he has never asked for. He has forgotten them.'

'We ought to find something there to suit my purpose.'

'If I take you it will be a violation of Mr. Steen's trust – ' She ignored Joe's attempt at denial and continued inexorably, 'You will please to keep it between ourselves, sir.'

'Of course. But is there any chance we may be seen?'

She dredged deep into the pocket of a stout under-apron and brought out several bunches of keys. 'No-one goes there now.'

'Not Mr. Steen?'

'It is the last place he would go.'

Perhaps if she had known how anxious Joe Rigby was to see those rooms, old Mrs. Brewer wouldn't have taken him. What she was doing was to her a criminal act, it must at least be dispassionate. She would have condemned Joe's curiosity as vulgar. She would have been wrong. Joe had never seen anything of Romney's except his name on a tree. All else had been bundled away or destroyed. For Joe he had taken shape in other people's minds and for Joe, at this present impasse, that was not enough. He needed to see for himself.

It was a part of the Priory he had wondered about once or twice, in fact could hardly avoid wondering about since it was on the south front where the best rooms would be. Mrs. Brewer unlocked, without any fuss, the door that led to it, although they stood in full view from that navelike corridor where Mr. Steen, Miss Barbary or anyone might be expected to appear. Perhaps she knew their habits; she was not guilty or on edge as Joe was. With the door secured behind them he gave a sigh of relief, whereat she reminded him grimly, 'Mr. Steen also has a key.'

So when the suite was unlocked and the door opened to him, Joe was still pre-occupied by what on earth he would say to Mr. Steen and Mr. Steen to him if they were discovered.

'I can't open the shutters,' said Mrs. Brewer, 'it might be noticed from outside.'

She switched on the light and they both stood on the threshold looking in.

Joe forgot Mr. Steen. He remembered the rest of the Steens only to realise that if he were set down blindfolded in any of the rooms at the Priory he would know which of all the family's was Romney's. Although he had never met Romney, although Romney was dead. Why? To know that, thought Joe, I should have to be analytical and profound. And then I should know but should not feel.

There was no describing how he thought he knew, either. He could say it was not a pleasant sensation, yet he could not say it was unpleasant. It was an intensification of that conflict which was to be felt everywhere else at the Priory. And here, in this room, something was added – a spurious passionate sweetness, as of self-pity.

Joe perhaps was contributing that, for the room was beautiful too, and it was the closest he would ever come to Romney in the flesh.

In these apartments, with their south aspect, centrally placed so as to look out over the best of the park, at a point farthest from the smell of the kitchens or the traffic of the Priory's daily life and devotions, was intended no doubt a lodging for the archbishop or cardinal. The proportions were infallible, serene. From the long windows, stopped now with shutters, the land and sky would spread away fanwise and the light reach into the plum-dark panelling. The wood had no depths now; dust and damp had bloomed it over; the same delicate fur was everywhere.

Joe looked at the silver-grey carpet, the juxtaposition of deep modern armchairs with Sheraton by-tables, frail and flaring; chrome-yellow curtains and a fireplace which would have stalled an ox; a Bechstein grand piano and an Ormolu clock, rich, fragile, absurd.

Hardly a boy's room – and yet, in a way, it was. The room of a boy beginning precociously to know what he liked in the mature world of the connoisseur.

There were other connoisseurs in whose mature worlds Romney had been interested. A sheaf of racing papers lay on a table, the top one doubled over to the three o'clock runners for Thursday, October 14th, 1948. Joe twitched it aside. Underneath were two paper-backs, puce and magenta-covered – *The Valley of Virgins* and *What Price the Lady?* Spine upwards between them and the race sheets was a slim scarlet leather volume laconically lettered in gold – 'Poems'. The pages were uncut, the quality of the paper promised a privately-printed edition. Joe turned it flat to shut it and caught a flash of green ink on the fly-leaf – 'To Romney, lovelier than life'. He closed the bent and unwilling pages and put it down with the Sandown Selections.

'Nothing's been touched,' said Mrs. Brewer, and indeed

the furniture stood raggedly about as if still askew from the shock of a year ago. Joe's gaze moved from one grained and tarnished mirror to another. There were five in all.

'Narcissus.'

Old Mrs. Brewer's fingers twitched with nausea; the dominion of the dust was a disgusting and debasing thing.

'I was forbidden to touch it,' she said. 'But I came the day after and set it straight. He was very untidy. He'd had his own valet for a year or more and I hadn't had to do with him. But I remembered the way he stepped out of his clothes, left them lying – ' Disorder or dirt she was not likely to forget. 'He'd been playing tennis and his white flannels would have been there now, on the floor of his dressing-room.'

At this outset of his connoisseurship, Romney had been clever enough to prefer the grotesque. It could be appreciated how beautifully the ugly monsters from China, the pot-bellied deities from the Solomons and one huge Hogarth print, rich and dropsical, had set off his own perfection.

A poseur. Where was Miss Barbary's 'warm-hearted and generous boy' in all this? Was there accommodation, between the five mirrors and the racing fixtures, for a 'heart of gold'? Joe wondered and as he wondered, came across something at odds with them all.

He picked it up, a small wooden picture-frame, home and painstakingly made. Each corner had been mitred off by a shaky hand, at one join there had welled up a yellow bead of glue. A bulky ivy-scroll was stencilled across the top. The sort of thing an unskilled lad would make with a fretwork set. Joe blew the film off it and took it to Mrs. Brewer.

'What about this?'

In her stout fingers it was more than ever gimcrack and frail.

'This was under one of the settee cushions. I found it when I tidied.'

'Why under the cushion?'

She didn't know. He'd been going to hang it up, perhaps, and it had slipped down there. He was very untidy.

Joe could not imagine Romney putting such a thing on his wall.

'Perhaps he'd been trying his hand at carpentry. It's very rough, but if he'd never done any before – '

Old Mrs. Brewer turned on Joe her direct stony look. 'He? That's Master Harry's work.'

'Then what's it doing here?'

'I don't know. The child was at it on and off for days. He went to no end of trouble but he wouldn't say who it was for. It was one of his secrets. Master Harry's a great one for secrets. This was the first thing he made with his carpenter's set.' She smiled faintly. 'I never knew him so proud of anything before.'

He'd made it for Romney and Romney jibbed at putting it on view among his ebony and jade.

So Harry *had* been fond of his brother, fond enough to labour at making a present for him. What had so suddenly provoked his hatred that it could outlast death? The reception of his gift? The scorn of it? Joe did not think so. It would be Romney's shortcoming which would have died for Harry.

'He was very popular, wasn't he?'

'He was.'

Joe, having asked the wrong question, had got the wrong answer.

'I mean – everyone loved him?'

Old Mrs. Brewer looked as if she would have liked to sit down on one of the dusty chairs. As her back stooped, the hatchet lines of her face grew harsher with what, in another woman, would have been tears. 'Young people don't know their power to harm.'

Joe recognised that she spoke to the outsider. But he was as sure as she was that her generalisation did not fit Romney. Romney had known his power to harm, his enormous exaggerated power, multiplied by his beauty, invincible because of it. Romney knew and relished and wielded it with artistry.

'We'd best be going. Is there anything here you want, sir?'

Joe picked up the picture-frame. 'I think I'll take this. It may help.'

She nodded but she was not thinking of Joe, she was not even thinking of Harry. She waited before switching off the lights, shrinkingly but deliberately laid her fingertips across the gritty panel of the door. 'It isn't possible he's gone.'

And in a fair way to being like this, perhaps she was thinking as she watched her fingers among the dust.

For the past ten minutes Joe had been watching Harry with his history primer. It was a new book with smooth strong paper, pleasantly printed and bound. Harry had been pleased with the look and feel of it even before he became acquainted with its contents. Now he had the corners of the pages in his fingers, bending, teasing and chafing them. He sat in his chair, aware neither of Joe nor the book. His restless hand was on the other side of the world from him.

'Harry?'

He gave no sign. Between his finger and thumb the corner of the page rolled into a tight cylinder.

'Harry!'

He looked up, but from such a depth that Joe shut his mouth on what he had been going to say. What was on the boy's mind was corrosive, as grief in a child could never be. His solitary air had more of the damned than the different about it. Like the pages of his primer, Harry Steen was being shredded away.

'Harry,' said Joe, 'these days when you don't like to learn, what is it you'd rather be doing?'

Harry wondered for a moment before enquiry changed to that blackness which was his infallible defence.

'I always like to learn.'

'I wonder what's stopping you.' Joe made it a statement to himself, not a question to Harry. 'You can't learn with half a mind and in your case it's no mind at all.' He opened the drawer in his table. 'I thought you might be wanting to get on with something else.' He took out the picture-frame and laid it in front of him. 'Carpentry, for instance.'

Harry's recognition took no time. It seemed to Joe that he had hardly lifted the thing out of the drawer before Harry knew what it was. One brief shock of fear as if, out of the blue, Joe had cracked a whip, and then Harry had his terrors in abeyance. Checked they were not; Joe could see what a prey he would be later. He saw something else which completed his mystification. Harry was relieved. In a joyless tired way, he welcomed what was obviously far more momentous than the mere reappearance of his handiwork.

'Where did you find that?'

'Never mind where I found it,' said Joe. 'You made it, didn't you?'

Harry folded his thumbs with one of his old-maidish gestures. 'I suspected you, you know. I suspected everyone. It seemed the best way because I didn't want it to come in the middle of anything. I might look as if I'd been caught. And I can't be caught because I haven't run away. I've been waiting for you.'

Joe braced himself. He was in the ticklish position of being supposed to know more than he did. If he could not uncover this obscurely sinister bee in Harry's bonnet now, he never would.

'Harry, I want you to tell me about you and Romney.'

The boy had been well-schooled in suspicion. His brows came sharply down. 'Why should I tell you if you know? You *do* know, don't you?'

'Of course,' lied Joe. He tapped the picture-frame. 'I knew when I found this. What I want is for you to tell me in your own words.'

Harry smiled, an ironic little smile. 'They always ask you to do that. I read a book about it, I wanted to know what to expect.'

Joe nodded, hopelessly out of his depth.

For Harry it seemed to be more than a solemn moment. He stood up and as he faced his tutor his fear, the abject monstrous fear of a child, threatened to overwhelm him. Standing there in the sunlight he was ready to drown. Joe's heart contracted with pity but he dared make no move to comfort the boy. It was the stern, almost punitive role Harry had assigned him which was prompting his confession.

'I'm waiting,' said Joe inexorably.

And Harry disciplined himself, once again put aside what he could not quell. His dignity would have looked comic to anyone who had not seen how hard it was to come by.

'Begin at the beginning, please.'

Harry began.

'I was making a present for my father. He was going away and I wouldn't see him for months.' Joe had never suspected that Harry selflessly, without return, loved his father. 'It was that picture-frame. I thought he could put a picture he liked in it and have it on his mantelpiece in the hotel where he stayed. It took me a long time to do because it was the first thing I'd ever made in wood. And of course it had to be properly done to go on his mantelpiece. My father,' said Harry, 'likes beautiful things. I was painting on the ivy when Romney found what I was doing. He said it was very nice. He said – ' Harry looked at Joe as if for reassurance on this point – 'that my father would like it better than a silver one from Asprey's. Then he took it away.'

'*He* took it? Did you want him to?'

'No. I tried to get it back but he said I wasn't to make a scene.' Unfamiliar colour crept into his cheek. 'He held it up and made me jump for it. I couldn't reach and then he said he'd get a nice picture put in it and would give it back to me ready to give to my father. He said he knew my father's taste in pictures.'

'And he never gave it back?'

'No. I tried to steal it back but he'd hidden it, and told Tass, his valet, to keep me out of his rooms. Every time I asked for it he said there was plenty of time. But there wasn't.' Some of the worry and desperation was still with Harry. 'The day before my father was to go away he still hadn't given it back. I asked him – he said he'd just got the right picture for the frame and would give it to father with my love. I said I wanted to give it but he said he could do it more gracefully.' For the first time Harry bent his head. 'I asked him what the picture was.'

'And what was it?'

His throat was so dry that Joe heard him swallow. 'He said it was – the backside of an elephant.'

Joe sat back with a sigh. So this was it. The teasing, ill-natured perhaps but thoughtless anyway, of an earnest homely child by his brilliant elder brother. It had made its mark, was bound to, and as the culmination of years of outstripping and unkindness, had confirmed an unforgiving hatred. It was a pity, but understandable in a boy of Harry's warmth. Precise and elderly though he sometimes seemed, he was still a child and had a child's difficulty in letting bygones be bygones. As to his fear, what was more likely than that all he hated and dreaded in his brother should in death seem doubly potent, almost almighty? 'A twig of a child' was not the only one to be shredded away by hauntings, real or imagined.

Thank God, thought Joe, at last I know what it's all about. I can deal with it, I can deal with Harry. I can even deal with Romney.

'Why, Harry, he was teasing you. He wouldn't have done such a thing – '

'Oh yes he would. He always did what he said. I knew he would and he knew I knew. He was playing tennis all the afternoon and I couldn't speak to him, but just before tea he went in and changed. I got past Tass and tried to look for my frame.'

'Did you find it?'

'No. They – he and Tass – both laughed at me. In the middle of it some wild ducks came flying across from the reservoir. He ran out with his gun. He ran into the wood to shoot them.'

'And then?'

'I followed and I killed him.'

The tall story, in the brief second of its impact, is always believed. Faced with Harry's hard matter-of-factness, it took Joe a further second to emerge from his shock.

'Harry, that's absurd – '

Harry wasn't listening.

'What I should have done was to have given myself up. If you hadn't come, of course I would have. But I wasn't really ready.' He looked down at his history primer and his fingers began to roll the corner of the page. 'I expect you've seen. I had to prepare myself. And waiting's been punishment.' So it has, thought Joe, remembering his aimlessness, the unhappy air of being no more than a bird of passage. 'I know it won't be very quick even though you've started. I can manage the day. If they shut me up I can count, but I have nightmares at night.'

'About Romney?'

'Oh no. About crying in front of the court and being chased by the hangman. It's not being chased that's the nightmare, it's the running away. I'm not sure of myself, you see.'

What Joe saw, looking into that small flinty face, was the irony of it. With something near despair he asked himself, how did it help that Harry's story was so patently absurd? Harry believed it beyond the power of ridicule or horse-sense to dissuade.

'You won't make a fuss, will you?' said the boy anxiously. 'When we go? My father will want everything as quiet as possible.'

So he will, thought Joe, and that's why you must be sure not to break down in front of the hangman.

Harry went to the window. He stood with his back to Joe and his voice was stifled as he pressed his nose against the glass. 'It's different already and it's only just begun. You're not what I thought the police would be like.'

'I'm not the police, Harry.'

He turned and looked. 'No,' he said slowly. 'You're not. You're – the Prosecutor, aren't you?'

Joe picked up the wretched picture-frame and shut it away in his table-drawer.

'Harry, you'd better go and get your lunch. There'll be no lessons this afternoon but I don't want you to be far away. Stay in the garden, will you?'

'You'll be taking me today?'

'Not today.'

Harry sighed, that same faint sorrowful breath Joe had heard before – of someone unutterably tired. 'I'm better when things happen quickly.'

Joe went to him, put both hands on his shoulders. 'Soon, I promise you, very soon, it will all be straightened out. I shan't let it take one moment longer than I can help.'

Harry moved from under his hands. 'I'll be by the mulberries till teatime. After tea I'll be in my room.'

Tutors are not provided with a supply of whisky for their own use or Joe would have poured himself a stiff drink. Of course he would have been justified in taking some of Mr. Steen's to help meet this emergency, but he disliked being lumped, if only in his own mind, with the butler who had been at the port.

It was as well he didn't take a drink because in half an hour he was needing another. During that time several unwelcome facts had presented themselves, making an absurd and horrible possibility a shade less absurd than it should have been.

The facts, as far as Joe had gone – which was farther, indeed, than he cared to go – could be set out like a row of beans. Joe's trouble was that they amounted to more than that.

First, Harry believed what he said and he had no reason for lying. Second, Romney was vaguely said to have slipped and fallen on his gun. More than that was needed to disprove Harry's story. Third, there was Mr. Steen's attitude towards his younger son. It could be explained, of course, by the poor showing the child made in comparison with Romney. But that argued indifference and the impression Joe had was not of indifference but of violent mental suffering. There was a split in Mr. Steen which was unaccounted for by grief. Could it be attributed to some reason, however slight, for suspecting Harry?

Harry might have spoken the truth.

'Nightmare at night?' said Joe. 'He's given it me by day.'

He tried ridicule. Eight-year-old fratricides keep to the Sunday papers. The mark of Cain is not a nursery rash.

Harry may be a twig of a child but if I believe this I shall be green as grass.

He tried reason. How does a child murder a lad of seventeen? How does he do it so that it shall look as if the lad shot himself – by accident? How, for that matter, does anyone arrange a murder by misadventure?

He tried retrospect. When young Robert Moxey told me his father was a Zulu chief, did I believe that? When the Blackstone boys blamed their booby-traps on poltergeists, did I give them the benefit of the doubt? And there had been another child who confessed to murder. Little Charley Scoe, taking the wish for the deed, declared he had killed his baby sister.

Why didn't I believe them? Why, because they didn't live in a monument; they had homes, not an inheritance.

Joe frowned at the bosses of thumbed stone. There was nothing of this to condition me, no architecture, no history, no weighty ghosts. From the beginning I've been fanciful about the place, acting like a tourist, reading the stones, gilding the lily – the Gothic lily – laying on more tragedy and mystery and violence than a hack scribbler would dare. I was ready for anything. Is it to be wondered at that I was ready for this?

So he blamed the Priory. He put Harry's story in its proper perspective and then he should have been ready for the real problem, that of dealing with Harry's undoubtedly tormented state of mind.

He was not ready. There was another reason why Harry's confession struck fear into him, one he had not advanced because it could not be demolished. The reason was Harry himself.

No amount of cheap fantasy could account for him. He was not an ordinary small boy – supposing there were such a creature. He was a fanatic. Far from being reassured, Joe understood for the first time how pitiless and predatory was the spirit that moved the child. The sin committed, he was prepared, he was waiting, to wither for it. His prayers were not for mercy but for strength to hide his fear.

Harry was capable of passions, not tantrums. Harry was – capable.

Chilled, Joe stepped to the window into a rod of sunlight. On the terrace he saw the grey figure of the boy, standing looking across the park. The wind flattened his hair, pressed his clothes on his narrow bones. He did not move. An aeroplane bumbled overhead. He did not look up at it. He stood for a long time before he went very slowly down the steps to the circular bench by the mulberries. He was going to be where he could be found.

How much longer can it last? thought Joe. He is stretched so tight a finger-tap will break him. Soon it won't need even that. He will snap, physically or mentally or both, and whatever it is that makes him neither Tom, nor Dick, but Harry Steen, will be gone for good.

Joe turned away. Knowing Harry's mind, it seemed, was only to know the size of the task. He could not even begin on the assumption that the boy was lying.

'What I must know is whether he *could* have done it.'

How Romney had died was not a question he felt he could ask any of the household. Mrs. Brewer, perhaps, but he would need details and she had a knack of closing up at any hint of curiosity.

He left word that he would not be in for lunch and taking his hat and stick, let himself out by the cloister door, thus avoiding Harry by the mulberries.

This was the first time since his arrival that he had been away from the Priory and when he stepped out on to the dust-floured lane he felt, guiltily, that he was stepping into a welcome change of air. What it was, more likely, was Joe Rigby feeling ground underfoot where he had been out of his depth so long. For as he came into the lane he remembered that this was the way the bus went between Bessemer and the county town and thought of the county town reminded him that there would be a local newspaper with offices there. Offices with files and back-numbers. And Romney Steen, heir to the Priory, be he only half as brilliant as he was made out to be, would rate at least a paragraph in the paper when he died. There would be too, an account of something else, something that was the due of the dullest and the most significant, should he end suddenly enough. The inquest.

So when the bus came, the same high yellow bus sinking tides of dust on the hedges, Joe was rattled into town.

A stranger wishing to look through the back numbers of a newspaper did not occasion as much interest as Joe feared he might. He had a dread of someone's coming to the same conclusion as his acquaintance in the bus on his journey down and taking him for a detective sent to rummage in the Priory affair. Besides, the last thing he wanted was for his interest to be reported back to anyone at the Priory. He was prepared to go to quite a lot of trouble by showing interest in anything else under the sun. But he was lucky. The lunch-hour was not yet over when he found the newspaper offices; even the desk-clerk had slipped out for a beer and the solitary boy in charge was less interested in Joe than in the orange he was peeling.

The back numbers of the paper were on battens in their chronological order and it took Joe very little time to find the issues of a year previous. It was a weekly paper and the report of the death was followed in the next edition by the report of the inquest.

Romney had merited more than a paragraph. He led the local news with two columns and a half. There was a photograph, the only one Joe had ever seen of him. It showed a young man, so much more of a man than a boy, standing with his gun under his arm at a local shoot. Handsome he was, the rough-grained print could not spot over that. One other attribute it revealed; his self-possession. In the fullest sense of the word, thought Joe, loving and possessing himself. Those large-lidded eyes, the idle graceful stance, were the outward signs of it. Joe could have sworn that here was one who did not make mistakes, who never endangered the comfort – let alone the safety – of his person.

He read rapidly through the reports of the shooting and the findings at the inquest, jotted down a note or two and left the building as the desk-clerk, breathing ale, came yawning back to his stool.

Joe went across the street, retracing the desk-clerk's steps to The Burning Glass, and ordered a late lunch of bread and cheese and beer. It was good fresh bread and nutty cheese, but he ate without enjoyment; he was at the same time savouring certain unpleasant details.

Romney had gone out, as Harry described, to take a shot at some wild duck which had flown into the copse. His gun was heard several times, then there was silence. He was found by a gamekeeper, lying on his face with the gun by his outflung hand. He had been hit at very close range by his own shot. There were tussocks in the copse, there was one by Romney's foot, there was even the imprint of his shoe on it. Anyone moving quickly, too eagerly, gun in hand fully cocked, anyone *could* trip and fall and, striking the trigger, blow out his own brains. Of that, the Coroner, with all the facts before him, had been satisfied. The verdict was 'death by misadventure'. There was no indication whatever that anyone else had been to blame, nor the slightest grounds – as the newspaper said – 'for suspicion of foul play'.

Recalling the tone of the reports, it occurred to Joe that this sudden blotting out of one so young and vivid and invulnerable had most severely shaken those who were older, dingier and more prone to disaster. And by the same token they had been glad that death was so impartial.

He waited in the Square for the bus back to Bessemer. Finding the answer to one question had posed another. Harry hadn't killed his brother, so why did he say he had?

Joe thought he could make a guess. Harry's warmth and affection, turned unwillingly to hate, must have amused Romney. So had Harry's unquestioning love for his father. Romney had exploited both love and hate, baiting 'Brother Rat' as a pastime. How often must Harry have wished him dead and how expeditiously was that wish granted when Romney at his most cruel, at the height of Harry's hatred, was mysteriously and terribly cut down. What could be more likely than that it should seem to Harry that the agency was his own ill-will?

He was fatally self-sufficient. He would be waiting at Bessemer now, his own judge, his own jailer and, given time, his own executioner.

Am I the only one who can stop it? Joe stood there, tapping his steel foot slightly with his stick; it was perhaps his timid self reminding him of his disability. That same self asked, alarmed, 'How can I accept such a responsibility?'

Mr. Steen had asked for him during his absence. In the lobby-like room which he used for conducting the business of the estate, Joe found him methodically writing cheques for a little pile of bills. He nodded to Joe and pushed forward a box of cigarettes. Joe took one and lit it and for a moment or two the only sound was the rustle of Mr. Steen's pen.

You are very like Harry, thought Joe; as like him as you were unlike the other. What flattery it must have been to have fathered the brilliant singular Romney, to know you were the source of those perfections. Whereas begetting dowdy little Harry was to perpetuate the ordinary in you. But whether you care for it or not, you had *two* sons and now one, poor devil, is damning himself. Can I help it? Who but you can undo the harm you've done him? You and your incomparable Romney.

'To-morrow,' said Mr. Steen, clipping each cheque to its corresponding bill, 'I am leaving for Brussels. I expect to be away a few weeks. You will have sole charge of Harry, do for him and get for him whatever is needful. I shall leave a blank cheque to cover any expenses.'

Yes, do that; tidy him away with your bills for sheep-dip and chicken-feed. Pin on a cheque and forget him. That's Harry Steen dealt with.

Such a wave of anger overcame Joe that he had to move to conceal it. He stood up and stubbed out the cigarette on the table before him. It rocked slightly under his violence.

Mr. Steen said, 'Is that satisfactory?'

'Quite.' Joe waited a moment before he went to the door.

41

'Goodbye.' He had it open, was half-way out when Mr. Steen asked, 'How is the child getting on?'

'It is a mistake to think of Harry as a child.'

'Is it?' Mr. Steen looked disbelieving. 'He is still very young. I felt that was why I could never approach him.' He crushed and rolled the edge of a tradesman's circular with a gesture which was the twin of Harry's. 'We could not trust each other.'

Joe said harshly, 'Harry's chief fault has been that he is not Romney.'

Mr. Steen's hands froze among the papers on his crowded desk. He did not look up. Joe, waiting for the pain to give way to anger, did not care if he were dismissed or not. But when at last he raised his head, Mr. Steen was smiling.

'His chief fault? It is his chief virtue.'

Joe looked at that wry gentle smile, could make nothing of it.

'Goodbye,' he said curtly, and came away.

He went in search of the boy. Harry was in the house-keeper's room, having his tea with old Mrs. Brewer. On the plate before him lay a slice of bread and butter with a hole picked in the middle. He looked up wildly as Joe came in and something which might have been hope changed to something that was unmistakably fear.

Fear now, of me, thought Joe. He sat down wearily and Mrs. Brewer went with a tray to the kitchen to fetch tea for him.

As soon as she had gone, Harry said, 'My father's going away.'

'Yes.'

'To-morrow – '

Joe nodded.

'I shall never see him again!'

'Hadn't you thought of that before?'

'Thought of it?' The absurdity of that bewildered him, but he was in too great a trouble to consider it. 'Does he have to go? I shall be gone so soon! Only a day or two – that's all I have, isn't it? Isn't it?' In a passion of grief he flung himself on Joe and beat at him with closed fists. 'I shall be hung in a day or two!'

Joe held him by the wrists, firmly but gently. 'No, Harry, whatever happens, or has happened, you will not be hanged.' The boy was ducking his head like a colt to knock away his tears, the first Joe had known him shed. Joe had great hopes that they would ease the intolerable emotional strain. 'You will see your father many, many times yet, Harry.'

Harry became very still. Then calmly, coldly, he moved his wrists out of Joe's grasp. He lifted his head. Joe, appalled, met his hard pitiless stare.

'There is such a thing as justice,' he said.

Joe was alone when Mrs. Brewer came back with his tea. He had his steel foot up on his other knee and was absently kneading the stump bone above the ankle.

'Where's Master Harry, sir?'

'Gone up to his room.'

She set down the tray and poured him a cup of tea. 'You look very tired.'

'Can you tell me why Harry is so fond of his father. He gets no encouragement.'

'A boy is always fond of his father.'

'He has no-one else, has he – apart from you? The loneliest child I ever knew.'

She pushed her sewing aside impatiently. 'What is to do? There's not a ray of happiness in him. He sat here as if he would tell me something and then he shut his mouth and wouldn't even eat. Look what a tea he made. Of course he never likes his father to go away, but this time you would think it was death to him.'

'And Mr. Steen has time only for the dead.'

She stiffened, sensing a reflection which was not permissible from an outsider. 'What do you mean, sir?'

'I mean,' said Joe bitterly, 'that if anyone is to blame for Harry's state of mind it is his own father. He has denied Harry everything – love, understanding, companionship, help – it went to the one who needed it least and now doesn't

43

need it at all. It isn't grief to idolise the dead and despise the living.'

'If he could idolise the dead he would be a happy man.'

'If he could? He does.'

She shook her head with the patient sorrow of the old. 'Not now.'

'Why not now? There's been no change of heart.'

She stood up, smoothed her glossy apron as a reminder to them both. 'You are mistaken.'

'I'm not asking you for gossip, Mrs. Brewer, I appreciate your reticence. But if anything is to be done for Harry, I am the one who must do it, and if there is any straw I must catch at it.'

Gathering the tea-cups and stacking them, she did not need to look at him. Her voice was harsh and unwilling.

'When Mr. Romney died, things came to light which Mr. Steen knew nothing of. Then he knew – what we all knew. No-one could save him that. He said, "He is better dead".' She turned on Joe her hard direct gaze. 'That is real grief.'

Opening his window to the dusk, Joe had a sense of respite for the second time that day. Just as, when he went through the Priory gates he seemed to lose a load, so now he looked across the shrouded park into a blessed timelessness. Not even the high maidish chime of the clock could impose a measure on that. Our time's our own; we made it and limited it to flesh and blood. The tides and the phases of the moon and the passage of the sun have nothing to do with it. Nothing, thank God, thought Joe, who, like all those who suspect themselves of failure, felt the tyranny of time.

He turned away and let the moths blow in through the open window and crackle round his lamp. Harry's days and nights had almost run out. The wonder was that his slight flesh and blood had stretched to so many of them.

Joe saw no chance of help from Mr. Steen. He was, if anything, more broken by his bitterness than by his single-minded grief, a man who had been disillusioned by the dead and could not bring himself to trust the living. Strength to found the relationship between father and son must come from Harry himself. Joe, with a Jewish gesture, threw up his hands and went to end the agony of a singed white beautiful creature thudding between the lamp and the shade. Not that he lacked faith in Harry. Harry was something of a giant-killer in his way; but he already had a giant on his hands. Conscience, a very bloody giant and no less so because it was misinformed.

So it falls to me, thought Joe, shutting the window to stop the martyrdom, to take a hand against it. And I have been afraid of that.

Because here at last is the opportunity to measure up, for once, to what I would like to have been. Easy and unimpressive it looks. To save the child I have only to convince him that he did not do a thing he could not possibly have done. Yet I would rather save him from fire or swim out with my steel foot to keep him from drowning. I would find that easier. And more spectacular. God help him – even I want to cut a dash.

Convincing Harry. Joe heard his own voice explaining endlessly. 'You see, Harry, you wished him dead that day. He was being cruel, he was threatening to insult your father so that it should appear the insult came from you. You believed he would do it, didn't you? You wished for anything to stop him, anything – even death. There was an accident and suddenly he *was* dead. It seemed as if you had wished his life away. It seemed to you that you must be his murderer. But you weren't, you couldn't be. Romney killed himself. Why, if all our ill-wishes were granted we should all be murderers. Romney was shot, he himself pressed the trigger as he fell. You do see, Harry, don't you, that you couldn't have done it?'

Harry would not see. The small flinty face would not change. In the dark of his own making all that Harry could see was his crime and its punishment.

It's no use talking. Harry knows he did it. Proof, infallible, irrefutable proof that he didn't, that he *couldn't* have done it is the only hope of shaking him. Hope? When I know neither how nor where to look? Joe flung himself on his bed, lit a cigarette and prepared to search . . .

It was not until Romney himself, in the black tights of a dark angel, came and offered to re-stage the accident of his death for Harry's benefit, that Joe realised his brain was past being constructive. And by then the great elms had begun to swim out of the broken white mist of morning. Joe turned his back on them and slept.

Wick, bringing his breakfast tray, wakened him at eight. Surprise at sight of Joe lying fully dressed on his bed was superseded by discretion at sight of Joe's face. Wick shut his mouth and prepared to retire.

'Has Mr. Steen gone yet?'

'He leaves in half an hour, sir.'

Pulling at his collar-stud, Joe wondered if Wick suspected him of drunkenness. When he got up he even felt a little drunk as if he were under the quickening influence of good wine.

The trees stood deep in their own cold shadow. An old horse, his shoes covered with sacking, was steadily drawing a great roller to and fro over the lawn, darkening it as he bruised off the dew. Joe watched with a pleasure that seemed out of proportion to the moment until he realised it sprang from that same sense of timelessness which had offered him a dishonourable retreat. And some odd fancy – for a miracle perhaps to solve his problem – made him wish for a sight of Romney in this setting which he had completed and adorned. Joe turned away, wondering at himself.

Harry was not in his room. The sheets were flung back over his bed, the clock on the table had its face turned towards the pillow as if Harry had watched the hands move through the night to the moment when his father would leave.

Joe hurried downstairs. The spurious detachment of tiredness had left him now; Harry was squarely in his mind and he was beginning to be alarmed. As he crossed the hall the car drew up ready for Mr. Steen.

Joe stumped out on to the terrace. He looked up and down

but saw no sign of Harry. Down the steps to the shrubbery he went and came out of the early sunlight into cold earthy shadow. He called. 'Harry!'

The ground retained its dampness here, even in the dryest summer. Joe's steel foot slid under him on the beaten path. Creeping and slipping like that, he felt clumsy and old. And the stone seat by the mulberries was empty.

'Harry!' The fear in his voice shook Joe. He heard the car starting and went scrambling back to the terrace like a startled crab. As he broke out into the sunlight he saw Mr. Steen leaning from the car window to give last-minute instructions to Wick. Harry stood in the shadow of the laurels, watching.

Joe was both relieved and angry. 'Harry,' he said sharply, 'didn't you hear me call?'

For a brief moment Harry took his eyes off his father and at the sight of his face, Joe's temper subsided. He put his hand gently on the boy's shoulder, such a narrow shoulder that his big hand covered it. 'Don't you want to go and say goodbye?'

'We have said goodbye,' said Harry stonily.

Mr. Steen leant back in his seat, the window was wound up and the car crunched gently forward on the gravel. It gathered speed, swam decorously into the green tunnel of the drive. Mr. Steen did not look round. Wick gave his sharp black shoulders a twitch and went up the steps into the house. Joe and Harry were left alone.

So I have let him go without knowing anything. I wonder, thought Joe grimly, if this is the unwisest thing I ever did.

Harry stood very still until the sound of the car had died away. From far overhead came the pure splutter of a lark. Harry pulled off one of the ugly spotted laurel leaves and launched it from between his fingers. It fell at his feet.

'Are we going?'

'Harry – '

He whirled round, gripped at Joe's cuff. 'Why don't you arrest me? Why don't you get it over with?' By comparison with those fierce clouded eyes it was the skin – china-white and shining – which was transparent on his bones. 'Why are you making me wait? Is it part of the punishment?'

'Harry, let's talk this over quietly – '

'I have nothing to wait for now. Nothing!' cried the child with a wail of despair that chilled Joe.

'Harry, listen to me – '

'You know I'm a murderer, you know I must hang – why don't you hang me? I said I killed him – isn't that enough?' He asked in a voice that was dangerously quiet, 'You believe me, don't you?'

Joe saw that it would be fatal to admit his unbelief. Like a man on a quicksand who takes the next step because he must, he played his only card.

'Confession isn't enough, Harry. I must have proof.'

'Proof?' It might have been a word he did not understand.

'Why yes, Harry. In a court of law, people's statements have to be supported by proof – evidence, it's called – something to back up whatever they are claiming. You couldn't expect a judge to take your word that you had committed a crime, any more than you could expect him to take the word of someone who said he hadn't – '

'Proof.' He rubbed at his cheek, wearily. 'Why didn't you say so before?'

Joe had a sudden pang of dread. He put out a hand and touched the cold leaves of the laurel-bush.

'Of course I've got proof,' said Harry.

It was really gallant, Joe's effort. Shaken as he was, he pulled himself together, conjured up just the right sternly official attitude. 'Very well, Harry, let me see it.'

The boy turned into the shrubbery. He trod lightly down the same slimy path, leaving Joe to make his clumsy crablike passage in the rear. As he floundered, Joe was asking himself, What am I doing? It was proof to shake him that I wanted, not proof to convince me.

His teeth closed hard on his lip as one foot slid painfully. Comic for a cripple, this path. There was nothing to hold on to – Something met his outflung hand. Harry's arm; the slight

48

spindle bone under the grey sleeve held and supported him while he regained his balance.

'It isn't far now,' the boy promised. 'We can go back another way.'

'Harry,' Joe held him when he would have turned to go on. 'What is this – proof you've got?'

'It's the gun I shot him with. That will be enough, won't it?'

Joe's hand twitched and fell from the child's shoulder. He took it as gesture of dismissal and moved on.

He did do it. He did it, after all.

Joe watched the grey figure until it passed out of sight round the bend. He was so cold that he began to chafe his own fingers for comfort. He foresaw Harry's end, left in these same ham-hands – over cautious, fumbling, incapable hands.

The boy's voice called impatiently and he went stumping forward, nursing his big wrists like a handicap.

Harry was waiting in a little clearing. When Joe approached he dropped to his knees and carefully turned over the brash of leaves and twigs beneath an ilex. The earth had the consistency of a moist pudding, it clung blackly to his fingers. He looked up as he reached one hand into a hollow under the roots.

'Sometimes I don't think you really believe me.' He withdrew his hand from the hole and got up from his knees. His eyes were wide with their curious lustreless warmth. 'This will prove it.'

Joe saw him standing there, a small rough-headed boy with draggled socks and a rusty toy pistol in his hand.

LOST JOURNEY

THE FIRST TIME I saw Gerda Charles it was coming up to the fifth of November and I thought now there's a first-rate guy fawkes. She was in an orange box on wheels, parked in the high street. It so happened that the sun, slanting between Woolworth's and Sainsbury's lit up her face. When she moved, nodded and grinned, I was shocked. I have no great reverence for life, there's too much of it about, but there has to be a line drawn. It ought to be drawn this side of Gerda.

She was like those things that hang out of church gutters – hooked nose, pop eyes and a great long tongue. She was looking up into people's faces and her tongue was darting in and out as if she'd lick them up and swallow them. What bothered me was how she fitted into the orange box which was small and square. So where were her legs?

A girl came out of Sainsbury's with a loaded carrier-bag which she dumped in the box on top of the old woman. A jar of pickled onions fell out, hit the pavement and smashed. Onions rolled under the feet of passers-by. The girl and the old woman laughed. She was pretty, the girl, in a Spanish or Irish way, plump, dark-haired, white-skinned and warm. Her blouse was open at the neck, I could see her throat down to her cleavage, yet it was raw weather and most people were well wrapped up.

I had nothing particular to do, Saturday morning being my free time. I was propping up the wall outside the Grapes, when they opened I would go in and prop up the bar. The girl and the old woman and the broken pickle jar were a bit of fun, that's all they were at that juncture. I wasn't the only one looking at them and smelling vinegar.

The box was fixed into an old pram frame. I watched the girl's very nice breasts bear down on the pram handle to get the cart moving. She bumped it down the kerb, not looking where she was going. A Telecom van screeched to a standstill and the driver yelled at her. She calmly pushed the contraption across the road, the old woman put up two fingers at the Telecom man.

When they reached my side of the street the girl had trouble getting the cart up the kerb. I went to help, it bothered me to see those breasts getting bumped.

'You want to take it easy, this is a busy road.' I lifted the cart by its front axle.

'And?' said the girl.

'You nearly got your mother killed.'

'My mother!' She put her hair back from her face and looked me over. 'Fat chance,' she said calmly. 'Give us a hand up the hill, will you?'

That's how I was caught up with those two. The girl's name was Lalla, if she had another I never knew it. Gerda told me once that she herself was a cousin of Robert Dudley.

'Who's he?' I said, and she said:

'The Earl of Leicester, the Queen's lover.'

'You could be the Duchess of Dillwater,' I said, 'but I never heard of any hanky-panky in that quarter.'

'On my mother's side of the family,' she said. 'Robert and I shared a wet-nurse. And it was Elizabeth Tudor, you bloody fool.'

That came later. As I pushed Gerda up the hill that Saturday I thought here's a turn-up for the book: I wonder what sort of book it was.

They told me they lived at Charlesworth Manor. 'My ancestral home,' said Gerda, with the cackle I now know so well. Charlesworth is a mansion set in acres of ground outside the town and it's been empty for years. They were in fact squatting there.

For reasons best known to myself, and not all connected

51

with Lalla – Gerda herself fascinated and repelled me – I pushed the box-cart up the hill and along the lanes and the length of the overgrown, bramble-bound drive and round to a side door of the house.

'You're blown,' said Gerda. 'A young fellow like you. I'd run rings round you if I had my legs.'

'Well you haven't,' said Lalla. She took the shopping out of the cart and by accident or design the blanket came with it and I saw that all Gerda had was a pair of rusty black trousers sewn into flaps where her legs would have begun.

Those two had broken and entered the house. Boards nailed across the door frame had been prised off and used to smash the glass panels. After that it would have been easy to reach through and pull back the bolts. I could see Lalla doing it, and Gerda egging her on.

'Suppose you're spotted?' I said.

Lalla shrugged; Gerda said amiably, 'There's more than one way of killing a cat.' I wasn't surprised, the idea had already penetrated that they could take care of themselves.

Certainly they could. They were occupying a room beyond the one they had broken into, which was a sort of scullery-outhouse, and they had made a bedsitter of what must have been the kitchen, a big vaulted place with built-in dresser and a range that would have cooked a horse. They had found three broken-down armchairs and stuffed the holes with newspaper.

'Two are Lalla's, the other's mine,' Gerda said. 'I don't need to stretch in bed.' They had the original kitchen table which was so heavy that no-one could have shifted it, a tea-chest for wardrobe and packs of paper cups, plates and air-line cutlery still in polythene wrappers. Lalla opened the door of the range on a clear, hot, liquid fire. 'Plenty of coke in the cellar,' said Gerda.

They told me to come again if I liked. I didn't know if I would like until Lalla took me out into the scullery and stood close.

'How do you manage?' I said. 'Heaving her about?'

'She can creep a bit.'

I went back the next day. The weather had turned unseasonably warm, a thick gold sun and leaves drifting down off the trees. I was on my motorbike, I knew the leaves would be falling in dead quiet and it struck me as sinister. Then I realised it wasn't the leaves and I nearly rode past Charlesworth. I wish I had, I wish to God I'd heeded the warning.

I turned into the drive, switched off the engine and walked the rest of the way. Somehow I didn't want to advertise myself, I suppose it was a bit of a defensive measure.

They were sitting outside taking the air, like a lot of people that last fine Sunday afternoon of the year. Gerda was in the armchair which also served as her bed, the castors had cut up the moss on the brick path when Lalla dragged it out. Gerda seemed to be asleep. Lalla was on her back on the grass, hands under her head, knees cocked and swaying to and fro, sort of lazily beckoning. She was a shape to dream of, I'd had many a dream about that girl before I ever saw her.

I propped the bike against a tree and crossed the grass. She had her eyes closed, she was smiling, lips parted to show the tip of her tongue. But for the old woman, one of my dreams would have come true then and there.

Gerda wasn't asleep. She says she never sleeps and I believe her. She may shut her eyes but she's watching, I swear I've seen the glitter of her eyes through her eyelids. 'What's that?' She pointed to my bike.

'A Yamaha Tri.'

'A motorbike? Can't you do any better?'

'It's not so bad.'

'It's no good to me.' I couldn't dispute that, nor could I see why I should. 'I need four wheels,' she said.

'A try-what?' said Lalla.

Her swaying knees mesmerised me. 'It's Japanese. 981 cc's, cush drive.'

'Why haven't you got a car?' Gerda's tongue came out too. I looked away.

'I can't afford to run one.'

'You know about cars? How to make them go?'

53

'Sure. You switch on the ignition and release the hand-brake.' It was my idea of a joke.

'Show him,' Gerda said. Lalla lay there, moving her knees. Gerda didn't raise her voice, she hurled it. 'Take him! Show him!'

'Take me,' I said to Lalla.

She raised herself slowly. When she stood upright her eyes blinked open like the eyes of a china doll.

'And me,' said Gerda, grinning.

Lalla smiled at my expression. 'Push the chair, it's easy.'

It wasn't. I was soon sweating, alternately shoving and dragging the armchair with Gerda in it, I thought any moment it would fall apart, Lalla led the way round the house, across a yard to some outbuildings which had probably been stables. When she dragged open one of a pair of double doors the roof tiles heaved like rats under a blanket.

'Inside,' said Gerda, 'get me inside.' I managed to push the chair over the threshold, nearly tipping her out in the process. I couldn't see much except the shape of something big against the back wall. 'Go on,' she said, 'it won't bite you.'

It was dark in there and smelled of winter, all the winters, no summers. Then Lalla stepped inside and either it was my fancy or she really did light up the place. I saw that the something big was a car. I went to it through drifts of dead leaves and broken tiles.

'Well,' I said, 'well, well.'

It was a Studebaker convertible, thirty to forty years old, cased like a tank, bullet-nosed, with an aeroplane mascot and chrome wing strips. It was cobwebbed all over, loaded with dust, the wheel rims squatting on puddings of rotting rubber, the hood reduced to canvas rags stuck to a rusty frame. I've seldom seen such a heap, even in the breaker's yard.

'Can you make it go?' said Gerda. I laughed, I still thought her capable of a joke. Lalla climbed on the bonnet among the bird-droppings and posed like the girls do at the motor-show. I fooled around, whipped open the driver's door. The car gave a groan and settled deeper into its rust. 'Make it go,' said Gerda.

Half a crazy old woman without a claim in the world on me, gave a totally ridiculous order and suddenly I was dead scared. 'Look,' I said, 'do you take me for a fool? Or a magician? This rubbish won't go in a million years.'

Gerda looked at me, not like a woman, even a crazy old one, more like a snake. All she said was, 'I can't wait that long,' and froze my blood.

I marched away down the drive to where I'd left my bike; if I knew what was good for me I wasn't coming here again. I sat in the saddle, my foot on the kick-start, then Lalla caught up with me. 'Do it to please me,' she said.

'You!'

'You could come whenever you fancied.'

'I wouldn't fancy.'

'No?' She pressed against me. 'Guess what it's like, alone with her, nothing to do, no telly, not even a radio. You could come in the evenings, we'd see each other as often as you like.'

'We can do that anyway.'

'In private, in there with the car.'

'What's she to you? Are you related?'

'God, no.'

'So why stay with her?'

Lalla has a way of buttoning her lip, childlike but not childish. 'That's my business.'

She was welcome to it. I wasn't drawn to her because of her beautiful nature and I didn't assume, as someone else might, that she stayed out of pity. I knew that she didn't stay as an act of charity or for any other reason. It was Gerda who kept *her*. And in my blood or my brains I sensed that I was in danger of being kept too. But Lalla drew me like a magnet. I took the risk, cocksure that I could handle it. And Lalla. I didn't begin to see that the dice was loaded.

I started going to Charlesworth in the evenings and working, pretending to, on the car. The first thing I did was clear out the back, and for a while everything went according to my plan. Lalla came to the garage and we had some very rewarding moments and knocked a lot of stuffing out of the back seat. The springs were still springy, the weather was mild, we weren't disturbed, and everything was laid on. Lalla was wonderful, the girl I'd always dreamed of having. I couldn't get enough of her. That, too, was laid on.

Then one evening she came late. I'd almost given up. Gerda, she said, was asking questions about what I was doing.

'Tell her we've been testing the rear axle,' I said.

Lalla didn't smile. 'Think she doesn't know?'

The next evening she didn't come at all. I waited, walked around the car, kicking it. For something to do, I tried to open the bonnet. The grips were rusted solid, I battered them free. Then I fetched the storm lantern which was all the lighting there was, and looked inside.

That engine wasn't a challenge so much as a black comedy. The battery had split and leaked. Only the fact that the car was built like a steamroller had stopped the acid eating through the wheel arch. Every bit of rubber was shrivelled, the wiring was scrambled, there was a bird's nest on the sump.

I started picking out the rubbish, dead leaves, beetle-cases, straws, and the next thing I knew I'd taken a rag and was cleaning off the rust. Next thing – you've guessed – I had started tinkering. But you won't guess how soon I forgot about Lalla. I worked, really worked, stripping that engine, until nearly midnight. When I say stripping, I mean simply stripping off the muck and frass of years. The next night I took solvents and white spirit and wire wool and a bundle of rags along with me. Just in case she doesn't come, I said to myself, I'll have something to do.

She did come. We got into the back of the car and I said, 'What happened to you yesterday?' Gerda had stopped her coming, she said. I nodded. 'Tied you to the kitchen table, did she? Or just knocked you out?'

Lalla said bitterly, 'Don't be so bloody naive.'

I was annoyed and didn't give her a chance to say more.

She left soon after, without another word. I hung up the storm lantern and started chipping out the remains of the battery.

I spent three evenings cleaning up the engine and I promise you I was never so hard to please. When I work on the bike I'm not fussy. I'll check the parts are back in place, the screws tight, maybe I'll wipe off excess oil and grease, and that's it. Believe it or not, I chipped, scraped, rubbed and worked on that old wreck, scrupulous as if I was cutting and polishing a diamond. I kept stopping myself to ask why. Who I was doing it for? I had the answer, I couldn't believe that either.

She came one night when I was on my back sounding the chassis with a spanner. I didn't hear her, just felt the prickle up my spine as if something crawly had got into my shirt. I looked out from under the car and there she was, in the box-cart, her beak nose aimed at me. I said, 'How did you get here?'

She showed me how she propelled herself by pulling on the wheels of the pram frame. What she lacked in strength she made up for determination. Doubled over in her box, head down, arms flailing, she was like something trapped under a bowl. 'Where's Lalla?' I said.

'Gone into town for fish and chips. To celebrate.'

'Celebrate what?'

'The car's ready, isn't it?'

'Ready for the crusher, yes.'

She nodded, she seemed pleased. 'I can't afford to pay you, but you can come to supper.'

I said, 'I may as well tell you, this thing will never go on the road again.'

'Tomorrow you can take me for a drive.'

'Not on your life.'

'On my life,' she said, and her face shone with a sort of Day-glo light.

I said, 'I can understand you wanting to get out for a change of scene, but if it means so much to you, you could hire a car. Because even if this heap could be persuaded to move, you'd be risking your neck in it.'

She grinned, showing big yellow teeth. 'The last time I risked my neck I lost my legs. I jumped in front of a train, I was desperate. Wouldn't you be, after five hundred years?'

'What?'

'Nice legs I had. I miss them. They're dead and buried, like all my best bits. You should have seen me when I was young and whole, at Cumnor. You wouldn't have had eyes for Lalla. Or Amy.'

'Who?'

'Amy – Amy Robsart.' She was at the age when the face suddenly gapes open and you see how it's going to look when only the bones are left. 'Don't worry about my neck, no one can take that. Or my life.'

'I won't be responsible.'

'Someone has to be. You or Lalla. I don't care which. Dying's a private privilege, you might think, but not for me. I've got to take a young one with me. That's the law.'

'Law?'

'Lex talionis.'

I said, 'I don't know what you're talking about. What I'm saying is that it would cost a packet to put this ruin on the road. It's over forty years old, it's American and it's rusted into the ground. It would have to have tyres, battery, brake-linings, cylinders, piston-rods, valves – just about everything needs replacing. It would be cheaper to hire a chauffeur-driven Rolls for a month.'

'I want to ride in this car.'

'I don't.'

She propelled her box-cart forward and hit the Studebaker with her fist. 'One last ride and then comes the snapping of the traces, the end of the gay and empty journey.'

I was out of my depth and the last thing I wanted was to get into hers. 'I'll go pick Lalla up,' I said.

I met her coming along the lane with a parcel of fish and chips. As she climbed on the pillion behind me I told her, 'Gerda's mad. You ought to get away from her.'

'I'll never get away.'

'You can go any time you like.'

'No.'

'Why not?' She was holding me tight round my waist, I could smell the fish and chips and feel the warmth of it pressing into the small of my back. 'Anyway,' I said, 'she's old, she won't live for ever.'

'No?'

'Look,' I said, 'there are these couple of things everyone has to do – get born and die.'

'Do you know how old she is?'

'Eighty, ninety.'

'She's four hundred and thirty-two years old.'

I twisted round in the saddle. It was too dark to see Lalla's face. 'Great leg-pullers you two. I suppose that's how she lost hers.'

'She can't die.' Lalla's whisper tickled my ear. 'She did something hundreds of years ago, murdered someone, she won't say who, as a punishment she's condemned to keep on living. Unless – '

'Unless she doesn't,' I said, and blipped the throttle so as not to hear any more nonsense.

Lalla shouted, 'You've heard of the Flying Dutchman!'

'That old film with Ava Gardner?'

'Film? God, you're crude.'

I won't say I finished work on the car, because I didn't do half what I should. I salvaged four tyres and a battery from the breaker, a friend found me some plugs. I reckoned if the thing didn't move it wouldn't want brakes, but I put in oil and petrol. The radiator pissed like a baby when I filled it. Never mind, I thought, it can't boil dry.

Every day Gerda asked was the car ready. When I told her yes, she stuck out her tongue, it might have been for glee but she looked like a lizard catching flies. 'Tomorrow we'll go for a ride,' she said.

The next day was a Sunday. I had a few drinks at the pub to set me up, then rode out to Charlesworth.

Gerda was ready and waiting in the back of the banger. Seeing her sitting there like gentry, bolt upright, her woolly hat on her head, I remembered what she'd said about being related to an earl. She scared me most when I thought she might be speaking the truth.

'Where's Lalla?' I said.

'Why do you always want to know where Lalla is? We don't need her. Drive away!'

'Not without Lalla.'

I kicked the front tyre which was bald as a coot. Gerda gave me a look which would have killed if she hadn't needed me alive. She banged on the side of the car. Lalla came out of the shadows and slipped into the front seat without a word or look in my direction.

'I can't take this on the road, it's not taxed or insured.'

'I don't care,' said Gerda.

'I do. It could put me in jail.'

'You needn't go on the road,' said Lalla, 'there's a cart-track that joins with the drive and goes for miles.'

Now I hadn't even attempted to start the engine, not out of curiosity or anything else. I had no curiosity about the wreck, it was just something I was lumbered with and struggling to get shot of. I sat behind the wheel thinking that with any luck the wheel would come away in my hands. I thought the ignition won't work, it can't, there's no circuit. 'Here goes,' I said, I sounded like my father when he used to play with me on the kitchen floor when I was small. I pulled out the choke, turned the ignition key and flattened the accelerator pedal to the floorboards.

If you know anything about motors, you're not going to believe this. There was an explosion and a sort of scream as if a rocket had been fired. That paralytic old engine started first go.

Panicking, I rammed in bottom gear and we moved with a noise like an iron foundry. Tiles, shocked off the roof, crashed all round us. We lumbered across the yard, I just managed to clear the wall of the house and we were on the drive.

If you know anything about motors you'll appreciate that the steering was diabolical. I needed to brace myself, feet on the floorboards, to hold the wheel – and I wanted my feet to operate the pedals. As soon as I dared, I changed up. The gears shrieked: something – power or fury or blue murder – belted through the chassis. The dead weight of rusty metal surged forward, we were away, breaking through under-growth, wallowing in and out of potholes, crushing fallen branches, careering over boulders, roaring and smoking. Like a rogue elephant. And about as tractable. I stamped the brake pedal down to the floor. Nothing happened. I pulled on the handbrake. There was a noise like tearing lino and a smell like a tar-boiler. The car shied slightly and kept on going.

I spend a lot of time now trying not to think about certain things: I try not to think about that ride. It took twenty years off my life, burned them off in minutes. I'll never be young again.

My only consolation, though I had no chance to savour it, was the fact that we weren't on the public highway. If other people's lives weren't at risk, ours were. I clung to that wheel, bracing my legs till they were ready to break, fighting to engage a lower gear and slow us down. I was sweating the slimy sweat of fear, my body slipped about under my clothes, as potent as a wet paper bag.

'Can't you go any faster?' Gerda was beating the back of my seat, in another minute I thought she'd beat me, ride me like a jockey. Her face in the mirror had that grinning glare.

'Can't you drive?' said Lalla. She too was smiling.

They had perfect confidence in me or they simply didn't care. Either way I was on my own.

The driveway had become a rutted track running through beechwoods. The trees, stripped for winter, had put iron-hard roots across the track. Every time we hit them at speed I expected we'd overturn, and burst into flames. I already saw the fire, heard my own screams. Suddenly I knew why Gerda reminded me of guy fawkes. She was programmed to burn, and me with her.

The track, which had been level, started to descend. The car picked up speed under its own weight. It seemed to exult. We swooped into blackness. I thought we were running through a railway tunnel. The headlamps, of course, didn't work. I prayed, 'Holy Mary, Mother of God – ' I'm not Catholic, it just seemed more hopeful to appeal to a woman.

'It's like the Tunnel of Love!' cried Lalla.

'Faster, faster!' shouted Gerda.

Then we were out into space, and light which was more than daylight. Even in the state I was in I knew it for the cold flat light off the sea. The awful din, the grinding and groaning of the chassis, the clattering of the doors and mud-guards and bonnet flaps, subsided a little, we were running across downland turf. But the engine was working itself to a frenzy. I prayed to Christ – a man might be better able to understand our situation – that it would blow up. I knew where we were – on Pendarrow Head. It's a narrow spur of cliff and we were belting across it to the sea.

I pumped at the brakes. The pedal snapped under my foot. I tried to get into lower gear and got into neutral. Sick with horror, I felt that bloody car leap forward like a greyhound out of the trap. Straight for a one-hundred foot drop to the rocks.

I didn't see Lalla get out. The next I knew, the offside door was batting to and fro on its hinges and the passenger seat was empty. I wrenched the steering-wheel from side to side to try to slow us. I wasn't reasoning straight, but I hoped if we turned turtle we just might stop rolling before we got to the edge.

That car wasn't going to slow and it certainly wasn't going to stop. If I wanted to live, I knew I had to get out. Fast. I let go of the wheel, ready to throw myself over the side. But I couldn't. I couldn't move. Gerda had me by the shoulders, she gripped me from behind with a strength I would never have credited her with. She was shouting in my ear, 'Faster, faster!' Maybe it was, 'Bastard, bastard!'

We came off Pendarrow Head at sixty miles an hour, me wondering how I'd die, feet up, or head down. It couldn't be too quick, it couldn't be quick enough.

As a matter of fact, I'm still waiting. We hit the water in a belly-flop, I remember seeing walls of water standing up all round me. Then came blackness, and roaring in my head, and the cold that kills. Death is everywhere at once – I found that out. Something was taking me down, and it wasn't only the weight of the car. I know now that it was Gerda. She had her hands on my shoulders, forcing me to go with her to the bottom of the sea.

True, the dice were loaded against me, but I have a life expectancy and I didn't mean to lose it to Gerda. I went berserk down there on the sea-bed, I bet they'd never seen anything like it before. I literally smashed my way out of the car, I broke off the steering-wheel and kicked in the dash.

But I couldn't get away from Gerda. Her fingers dug into my bones. I carry the marks of her nails to this day. It was the car that saved me. The bottom fell out, I was sucked down, torn out of Gerda's grip by the weight of the engine.

They say you surface three times before you die of drowning. The hell you do. I came up just the once, and if I'd gone down once again it would have finished me. When I got the air in my lungs I drank it, swallowed it, scoffed it wholesale. Then I struck out with arms, legs, everything I had.

What I had was mostly panic. I was scared of drowning and scared rigid of drowning with Gerda. I knew that she was somewhere underneath and it wasn't the sea clawing me back, it was her.

The tide was in. It rolled me to and fro like a lump of bladderwrack, for anyone watching it must have been a laugh a minute. Somehow I got a footing on a knife-edge of rock. Next minute it sheared into my chest as I was flung down. But I held to it for dear life, and when the waves screeched back over the shingle I got my knees where my hands were. While the next waves swamped over me, I clung on, when they receded I crawled over the rocks to the beach.

There wasn't time to rest. The sea was licking at the base of the cliff. In the high days of summer, picnic parties, kids with buckets and spades, Lilos and rubber dinghies, frequent this beach. A path has been cut into the cliff for their convenience. And mercifully for me.

I scrambled up it. I wouldn't want a dog to feel like I did

then, soaked to the bone, sea – or tears – leaking from every pore. My breathing deafened me. I dragged myself up over the cliff and fell on my face.

I could have died there, I wouldn't have minded dying on my own. The bitter wind sweeping across the headland, and something else – a feeling that I was watched, got me to my elbows. I propped myself on my arms and looked around.

Lalla was reclining on the grass a few feet away. 'You might have killed her,' she said.

I managed to croak, 'What about me?'

'It was what she hoped.' Lalla was eyeing me with distaste. 'God, you're a mess.'

I said, 'I nearly drowned, I'm half dead, and she's all dead – '

'Fat chance.'

'What?'

Lalla pointed out to sea.

I'll be able to see what I saw then till the day I die, whether my eyes are open or shut. I see it now. The old car was floating – yes, floating right way up – just beyond the rocks. In the back sat Gerda. She took off her woolly hat and waved it.

'Mother of God! – ' who else could I say it to? – 'She's not drowned!'

'Of course not,' said Lalla. 'You didn't stay with her.'

'Stay with her!'

'You were meant to. She was all set to die, but she can't unless she takes someone with her.' It wasn't distaste Lalla was eyeing me with, it was dislike. 'Someone young, lover-boy.'

JUST IN TIME

'ASHES TO ASHES, dust to dust.'

No, not dust, thought Adelaide, Dick would not have dust. Ashes were the product of something lively, something fierce, but dust was one remove from dirt, and lay about on the sideboard. Dick wouldn't have had these flowers either, cut off in their prime, he liked things to be growing, going on. He would suffer when they wilted and died on him. Perhaps she ought to remove them after everyone had gone? She suggested that they be taken up and sent to the local hospital.

'Wreaths? Crosses?' her mother said. 'I hardly think.'

'You mean they might give sick people the wrong idea?'

'My darling, what can I say?'

It was the question they all asked, but when no answer was forthcoming they did not relapse into silence, which Adelaide would have preferred.

'This, our dearly beloved,' murmured the priest.

'Never a truer word,' whispered Aunt Emmy, taking Adelaide's fingers between her new black gloves which were made of some plastic material, soft and limp like two small dead animals. Dead, like Dick. Adelaide snatched her hand away.

'Oh dear . . .' moaned Aunt Emmy.

'It's all right, Auntie, really.' It became Adelaide's task to console her aunt who went in mortal dread of saying the wrong thing and therefore often did say it.

Adelaide was wondering if she herself had *done* the wrong thing in not having Dick cremated. They had never talked about such matters: he didn't approve of death, was openly

65

sceptical of it. And she had thought him like the quick brown fox, slender and vivid and a trifle wild. 'My beautiful fox,' she had thought longingly, but without much hope, the first time she saw him.

Burning or burying – either way was horrible, but burning would have been quicker. She raised the question as they got out of the car at the churchyard gate.

'It did not occur to me,' said her mother, 'your mind seemed quite made up.'

'It wasn't made up, it was dormant. I could change it.'

'It's too late now!' Her mother sounded shocked, even scared.

'So is almost everything.'

'You've been so brave. I worry that you've been too brave, repressed too much. But now isn't the time to give way. Try to hold on just a little longer.'

'Though not quite everything,' said Adelaide. 'And I wish it had occurred to you.'

'Darling, pull yourself together – '

'I am together.'

'Of course. Nothing can change that.' Her mother, understanding, understood not quite all. 'You will always have him with you.'

'He never liked hanging about.'

'We are here to pay our last respects. It will be heart-rending but it will soon be over.'

One heard of people changing their minds at the altar but never at the graveside. Adelaide turned away to conceal the smile which Dick would have shared.

So they stood round the hole which, though neatly shaped and lined with what looked like greengrocer's baize, was no more than a hole with Dick in it, down at the bottom, inside an elegant polished box with a brass plate over his chest, tendering his name, Richard Quin, and his lifespan, 1957–1984. Not long.

Someone peripheral, a witness to the accident, had said, 'He had hardly started to live.' It was kindly meant, but untrue. Dick had set about living as soon as he was born, and would have insisted on his birthright while in the womb. He had made the utmost of the time allotted him. For Adelaide it had been like being in a race, a three-legged one.

Exhaustion she did not feel, only a sense of *déjà-couru*. 'Everything is so *stale*!'

'I can offer you some hope, darling,' said her mother. 'The feeling will soon pass.'

Adelaide said she could not accept credit when it was not due. 'I keep thinking "Not again!" and I haven't been to so many funerals.'

'I think we should pray.'

People were bowing their heads. Aunt Emmy held up her face and her hands in their new gloves, palm to palm. Such trust from such an old woman brought tears to Adelaide's eyes.

Her friend Margo asked, 'What will you do?' It was a cry from the heart and Margo had a very large heart. Dick said it was so widespread you ran the risk of cutting her to it if you accidentally jogged her elbow.

Adelaide, who had decided to do her own kind of nothing, said 'What can I do?' as a question for Margo rather than to get an answer for herself. She wanted to know what Margo thought she could do.

Poor Margo was wearing a quite unsuitable necklace, suitable to the occasion or what Margo saw as the occasion, but definitely not suited to her, for she was a soft, palpitant blonde and the double strand of fiercely faceted jet beads looked like some sort of penance round her plump throat. As was to be expected, her face crumpled. Ordinarily pretty, she now looked like a pretty gargoyle.

It was wonderful, thought Adelaide, how the human face disorganised itself in a certain inexorable sequence when confronted with the possibility of a change for the worst. And then she thought – not along her usual lines – that although a baby could do it, it was still a complex and highly specialised operation. 'It's a good thing we didn't have children.'

'Good? But you would have had help, the Government would have helped, there's family assistance and national allowances and you would have had something of Dick.'

'I have something of Dick.'

'You were like two halves of a whole!'

Adelaide sighed for reasons known (though not best) to herself. She had still to examine and assess them, it had not so far been possible to do that. While Dick was still alive it would have been disastrous and a treachery.

'When I lost my grandmamma, I went as cold as ice all over. Oh I know it's not the same,' wailed Margo, 'it doesn't bear thinking about, but if I was cold for my grandmother what are *you*?'

'Rather tired,' said Adelaide. 'And I should like some answers.'

'Answers?'

'To so many questions.'

'And you're not sleeping – '

'On the contrary, I go off as soon as my head touches the pillow. I always have.'

Margo's eyes widened painfully. 'A blessing.'

'Dick doesn't – didn't – sleep easily. He said I died when I got into bed.' Adelaide, who had been about to say that it presented problems, smiled instead.

Margo's face virtually dissolved. 'Addy, there aren't any answers to the questions you want to ask.'

'I don't want to ask, I'd just like to be supplied with answers to what *I'm* being asked. People do need telling. I suppose they think if they know what I am, they know what they can be. The trouble is, I'm nothing to speak of.'

'You mean you're numb?'

'There you go, asking. Oh, it would be easy if I were numb. I could be pushed into the right positions on the board like a chess piece, and everyone could get on with the game. But I'm not numb. I feel everything.'

It was true that she felt some things which she was really not entitled to feel at this juncture, and others which she was not entitled to feel at any juncture. But Margo would not insist on an analysis, she was too vulnerable herself.

Margo did in fact take refuge in her own emotions and cried reproachfully, 'You were made for each other!'

It had been the consensus of opinion. Not only among the romantic and sentimentally inclined: people who were themselves disparate and doubtful of finding their other halves were quick to declare that it could be done, and to point to the Quins who had done it. A union of hearts, minds and bodies: pegged, rabbeted and dovetailed some said, and let no-one put them asunder. Had anyone done so, he or she would have been reviled and detested. In a faithless and fluxional world, a couple like the Quins were cherished.

Adelaide could remember first hearing it said, the actual moment. She had the impression that it had been said before, just out of her hearing. The words were harmless enough: 'Ain't they jest the perfect couple!' She heard them again now, coming across a busy room with the honied drawl of the American deep south. Her mother's hairdresser, Beulah, speaking over the buzz of the driers as she watched Adelaide go to join Dick who was waiting for her outside. Adelaide had laughed about it to her mother who had said thoughtfully, 'You know, I would have expected Beulah to say you were the "cutest" couple. But she recognises the distinction. You and Dick *are* perfect together.'

If Adelaide had sensed an insistence, it was only to be compared with the tone in which her mother used to say to her as a child, 'You are to wash your hands and come to the table.' Afterwards she had recalled the tone of voice just as she recalled Beulah's, and felt no unease. Because at the time she believed that she and Dick were perfect for each other. They both believed it. Without conceit. Their perfection, they would have said, was private and personal, a one-off. They did say to each other that they were supremely lucky, and privileged, and they acknowledged – paying tribute out of sheer superstition – that fate, or the gods, or whatever, had favoured them.

One day they found that it was confidently expected that

they would make the perfect marriage. It went, it had gone, without *their* saying. Everyone else said it for them. Adelaide, on the crest of overmastering happiness, accepted it as the logical outcome of their perfection. Dick teased her and said they might have to work at it, and they decided that in that unlikely event they would never, ever, let the other one see that it had been necessary to try. So little effort would be required: with them, giving and taking was a mutual function and went on all the time, along with their breathing.

'Shall I stay with you?' said Margo. 'I expect I could manage two or three days.'

'No, thank you, my mother's staying and really it's not necessary. I mean, I have to get used to it.' She had put a little too much gusto into that and added hastily, 'We were warned.'

'Warned?'

'By that bit about "till death us do part".'

Dick and Adelaide were married at St George's which, besides being their parish church, was pretty and old. The little square tower, wearing a kind of witch's hat for a roof, had fairly rocked to the sound of their bells. It was of course a proper turn-out, with bridesmaids, gentlemen ushers, an organist, a choir, banks of stephanotis and Boule-de-Neige roses, an ivory-coloured Rolls, a four-tiered cake and crates of Pol Roger.

Adelaide and Dick had considered why such a wedding should be called 'white'. Adelaide said that the bridegroom's morning suit was equally worthy of note and the colour would have suited her better. They had toyed with the idea of a switch: Adelaide to be in dove-grey and Dick in duck-white. He maintained that he was no less virginal than she.

In those days they believed that they spoke the truth to each other – they did not suspect that there was in fact no definite article.

'My mother cried all the time I was being married,' said Margo. 'I could hear her.'

'Mothers are supposed to cry.'

'But mine snuffled!'

'Your wedding was in November and it was cold.'

'Yours was in April and the sun came out.'

'And we saw the cherry blossom on the way to Gatwick.'

'We were stuck at Heathrow for eight hours because of fog.'

'We – ' Adelaide paused. She had been about to say that they had seen the Alps by moonlight, but it was precisely the sort of thing which had perpetuated the legend of perfection – 'we had an uneventful flight.'

She went to the window. Margo made her restless, sitting there like a squashed pie. Why should Margo feel squashed? 'Let's go for a walk.'

'A walk?'

'There's a meadow on the other side of the railway full of buttercups. Think of it, nothing but thousands and millions of gorgeous golden buttercups. I saw them from the train. You never do nowadays.'

'Never do what?'

'See buttercups. So many. I want to go to them.'

'I'm not dressed for walking.'

Margo was dressed for a funeral, or her notion of it: peep-toed shoes, stiletto heels – black, of course; a black granny shawl over a charcoal suit, a Tam o'Shanter placed, not rakishly, on her puff of back-combed hair, and those spiteful jet beads. Adelaide found it frightening because, whether he liked it or not, it was part of Dick's epitaph. Everything that happened now must be whether he liked it or not.

'Why do you want to walk through buttercups?'

'I don't, it would spoil them. I want to go and look at them before it's too late.'

She and Dick had seen the buttercups the day before he died. They were coming home on the 5.40 from Victoria. Adelaide had cried out and leaned from the window to keep the flowers in view. *Financial Times* and *Evening Standards* were lowered, their fellow-passengers stared at her. Dick had considered that she was making an exhibition and when she turned back to him, babbling about a field of gold, he told her that it had been sold for building lots and bulldozers would soon tear up the buttercups. He didn't like the idea either, but he needed to be revenged. They could still acknowledge each others' motives, that habit, or faculty, remained.

Time had been when, however physically apart they might be, Dick at his City office, Adelaide at their bungalow in Belmont, they had lived and breathed in supreme consciousness of each other. There was not a moment of that time when they were not together. Their strength and serenity gave them an implacable innocence which some people found unnerving. To others, it was an inspiration. Simple souls like Aunt Em worshipped from afar, but everyone believed – or jibbed at believing – that Dick and Adelaide were indissoluble. Dissolution, when it came, obliged them to deny, individually, without letting on to the other, that they had ever, could ever, have been so close.

'I told you Harold couldn't come because his department's being investigated today, but he said something about Dick, he said, "He went while he was shining".'

'Like the buttercups.'

'It's not the sort of thing Harold says!' cried Margo.

'You mustn't worry.'

'I can't help it, everything's so awful!'

'It's really not.'

'You're being *brave*!'

'Nothing lasts.' Adelaide had meant it consolingly, but Margo's face was already sympathetically crumpling. 'Nothing perfect lasts. Though perhaps,' she felt no bitterness, 'the imperfect lasts a bit longer.'

That was something else Dick had said, a long time ago. They were on the beach at Katrinos where they had gone for what was to have been their second honeymoon. Disregarding indications to the contrary, they had fully expected, and indeed required, it to be an exact repetition of their first. 'Nothing lasts,' Dick had said. 'Have you noticed?' Discontent, as huge and vague as fog, came down on them. They did not immediately attribute it to themselves, they blamed the sea for not being so warm or so limpid as they remembered, and an itinerant pizza-seller who was causing the beach to smell like a Wimpy bar.

'You'll carry on,' said Margo, 'to the very end. That's something I could never do, even if I'd had it. Especially if I'd had it.'

'Had what?'

'A perfect marriage.'

It had been said so often, yet Adelaide, who had subconsciously been waiting for it to be said again, was stung, pierced almost to the heart. She and Dick had not fought because a fight took two, and her quietude, which had been the natural counter to Dick's vivacity – had contained and even endowed it – made her a non-combatant. Yet she was in no way submissive. Gradually it became clear to her that what she felt was alienation. And when Dick danced with rage she had smiled, as she might at a bobbing balloon.

During their second honeymoon they realised that they were lumbered with a perfect marriage, without themselves being perfect. It was a crushing blow. They had not wanted excellence, only to be right for each other. Adelaide recalled a line from a poem which put the question very nicely: 'Have I not been to you as the brown nut to the hazel?' The answer, though she had not put the question to him in that or any other form, came in Dick's voice: 'Nothing lasts.'

Those were the only words that had passed between them on the subject, on the beach at Katrinos. They left that impermanent place the same day and went on a boat tour of the islands. Nothing they saw comforted them.

'It was the purest luck,' said Margo, 'you finding each other. I mean, you could look and look and end up old without getting it right.'

'I wasn't looking, neither was Dick. We met and sort of interlocked.'

It was right for how long? Who could say? The moment, which had been all the while coming when their marriage would cease to be right, had arrived unannounced, almost unnoticed.

'Interlocked,' said Margo, 'and now you're torn apart.'

Every crease of her skin glistened. She was a little late with her sorrow, because the moment which had sundered them had arrived years ago.

The question had arisen, though by then it was academic, whether their marriage could ever have been right. Let alone perfect. Perfection was asking too much and was an enormous conceit which people who could not cherish it about themselves would do so about somebody else, thus keeping it within the bounds of possibility – which it was not.

Adelaide and Dick, who had been able to talk, and had delighted in revealing their congruent selves to each other, could not admit that it was all illusion. They could not own, to each other, that they were in the same overloaded boat as everyone else. And they certainly could not let anyone else know it.

Adelaide asked herself why, if no such thing as the perfect marriage existed, they should have to pretend that it did. Was it out of pride, or charity, or was it like Christmas and Easter, something to be kept alive for commercial reasons?

'I mean, God knows – or damn well ought to – ' Margo said fiercely, 'that there are plenty of lousy marriages to break up without picking on a good one.'

There had been times when they feared that their disenchantment must surely show. Singly, they could conceal it. Adelaide kept her mouth shut, often she had to bite her lip, and she knew that Dick did too. They were loyal, it went without their saying that the beans, if they were spilled, must be spilled fairly, and in the presence of each other. It was when they were together that the danger of spillage was greatest. They provoked each other. They were, after all, perfectly adapted to that.

The beans were not spilled because nobody wanted to know. It was accepted that there would be miniscule misunderstandings, kissing and making up was part of the perfect marriage. The idea of radical differences was unacceptable and tedious because it meant that something like the billionth-zillionth marriage was on the rocks for the same old reasons. Most people had tedious thought processes of their own to cope with, and found it cheering, and convenient, to keep their faith. They must also have found it fairly easy, for even the sceptics weren't sure about the warning signs.

Once, Adelaide's mother had asked her, out of the seeming blue, 'Is everything all right?' Adelaide, startled and alerted, needed time to check her defences. 'What do you mean?' Her mother said, 'Don't *pounce* dear.'

So far as Adelaide could tell, she had shown no chink, made no slip, she had been thinking, and talking, about whether they should have the bungalow painted. What she hadn't taken into consideration was her mother's concentrated and informed perception. Mother, it could certainly be said, knew best.

She had countered, aware of the enormity of the question, 'What could be wrong?' Her mother said, 'I was thinking of you. You were going to start a family, you said, as soon as you were married. It's three years now. Of course,' her mother blushed slightly, 'it could equally well be Dick's fault.' 'Couldn't it just,' said Adelaide. It was the nearest she ever came to owning that everything was not all right. The burden of proof was heavy, they were required to answer not only for an imperfect marriage, but for presuming that they had had a perfect one. Guilt was compounded by deceit. Why couldn't they take advantage of living in a liberal age and admit their mistake? Other people did. That, of course, was why they couldn't.

Dick had joined a club where he was unknown and his reputation as a happily married man did not precede him. He went there most nights after work and came home to sleep. They occupied separate rooms: Adelaide stayed on in the double bedroom at the front of the house, only Dick's hairbrushes on the dressing-table and his spare dressing-gown shared it with her.

Some nights she lay awake wondering if he would come, and what she would do if he did. That question, too, remained academic. As time passed they became so stiff-necked that their mutual embarrassment would have overruled any other feeling they might have had. Dick, she thought, looked at her with distaste. She thought that his flesh disclaimed her when they were obliged to link arms, hold hands, touch each other for the sake of appearances. A kind of qualm, starting in the air, went through them both as punctually and simultaneously as desire used to.

'It's our loss, too,' said Margo. 'I know what my father meant when he said the lights were going out.'

'What?'

'He used to say — ' Margo drew a breath, she thought she was striking the right note — 'one by one the lights are going out — '

'All over Europe.'

'It's got darker in Belmont!' cried Margo.

Adelaide found herself between laughter and tears. To hide the laughter she took Margo's hand and held it to her cheek. Oh Dick, she was thinking, you left it all to me, you died and left me the ghost of our perfect marriage.

They couldn't have kept it up for the rest of their lives if both their lives had been the normal span — and they had no reason to think otherwise. She tried to remember what she had expected. Had she hoped that things, even one small thing, might change? Not back to the way it was, but just for the better?

'Buttercups are perfect, ghosts aren't, but I daresay even they don't last for ever.'

'Ghosts?'

Then she thought — death had made her scrupulous — 'nothing lasts' also, and ultimately must mean that the state of nothing, the null and void bit, did last.

'That's right,' Margo said, weeping herself, 'you have a good cry, it's the best thing you can do.'

ELEMENT OF DOUBT

'BY THE BY,' said Hopcraft, fidgeting before getting up to go, 'what about Midgeley's paper?'

'What indeed.'

'You have it, I presume?'

'It is in my possession, yes. How much do you know of it?'

'Nothing. Midgeley spoke once of possibilities undreamed of, I was going through a bad bout of insomnia at the time and any dreams would have been welcome.'

'I doubt if Midgeley's are dreamable.'

'He hinted at profound implications.'

'He was certainly in over his head. I'm not questioning his intellectual stature, which we know was considerable. But I fear that in his last illness he was in an incendiary situation, febrile and possibly hallucinatory. He was over-reaching.'

'In what direction?'

'I can only describe it as a leap in the dark, accompanied by the sort of hyperbole no scientist should adopt. Speculation merely.'

'He was a reliable worker in the field. I would not expect him to cut corners.'

'His last exercise seems to me like a try for a raison d'être.'

'There is an element of doubt?'

'You could say that.'

'I take it you will not refer to his paper?'

'It would only diminish his reputation. But let me read it to you.'

Hopcraft looked at his watch. 'Not now, I have a meeting with the dean. Sent me a transcript.'

When Hopcraft had gone, Irving set about putting the pages of his contribution to the Cardew memorial lectures in order. He had typed them here on the College machine because of trouble with the line-hold on his old portable at home.

His piece was sound and predictable, he wasn't breaking new ground. To be honest, which he hoped he was, he found himself without any new ground. It was a recurrent situation and one had to conceal it, for one's own good and that of the establishment.

Midgeley's paper was in fact not here in college, but safely at home. There was something *un*safe about it, a veiled general threat which Irving felt he should analyse. If analysis was possible. He was conscious of a marked reluctance to read it again.

Irving placed the tips of his fingers together in a thoughtful gesture and intoned: 'It is an honour to be invited to contribute to these memorial lectures – ' No, better be casual, some people would be aggrieved at not being invited. He stood up, plunged both hands in his pockets and stooped smilingly as to an audience of friends. 'This isn't the first time I've contributed to the Cardew lectures, but it's still a great occasion for me. Tonight I want to talk about the proliferation principle.'

A nicely non-committal subject which would take him a long way without the obligation to arrive. It was open to question – this too was a recurrent situation – whether there was anywhere to arrive. He lacked Midgeley's faith. Midgeley had held to his belief that there was an answer. And at the end, believed he had found it.

Irving had known him from their schooldays. As a child, under-endowed, Midgeley cried 'Why?' when other boys punched him. It was the need to know exceeding his distress. At the end it had exceeded his reason.

Irving wadded his lecture notes into his overcoat pocket and went home.

*

In theory his children waited up to say goodnight to him. In practice it was Alice, the nursegirl, who waited. Caspar and Candida were asleep, Caspar with his thumb in his mouth, Candida crossly clutching her pillow. Alice sat on the nursery floor, surrounded by the children's toys. She was actually sitting on a pink and white rabbit and the rabbit's glass eye looked up from under her generous rump. She looked up at Irving, her eyelashes spiked black by an unskilled hand.

It had become a subject of mild amusement between Irving and his wife that the girl was besotted. She made no secret of it. In her early teens, plump, steamy and heavy-breathing, she breathed most heavily in Irving's presence. He had remarked, in her hearing, how draughty the house had become. She remained unaware that it was a joke at her expense.

She sat there now, on the rabbit, gazing at Irving and melting. She could be seen to melt, warm beads welled out of her pores and dried on her cheeks like dew. Irving thought she must be the purest thing in the house, not excluding the children who were tarnished with his own genes.

He nodded to her, smiled, and kissed his unconscious son and daughter. It was what he had come to do, though something was due to the girl. She was waiting.

'Have they been good?' They hadn't, judging by Candida's scowl. He picked up an engine from the floor. One of the wheels fell off. 'Dear, dear – ' Oxygenated, Alice half rose from the rabbit and for a second he feared she thought he was declaring himself. He hastily tossed the toy into the playbox. 'These things are inexcusably trashy.'

Her face was like a diagram face, without a single identifying mark, save for the blacked eyelashes. They, indeed, had congruity, as if they were the beginning of something else. Irving might have stayed to figure it out, but there were people coming to dinner.

'The Boldertons. They're new friends. I don't yet know if I like them. I certainly don't know if you would.' He was surprised to hear himself say, 'I can't ask you to join us.'

'You mustn't worry about me.'

79

He gave her a friendly wave as he went. But there was something in his hand – Caspar's broken engine.

'That girl takes too much on herself,' Irving's wife, Helen, said as they were undressing that night.

'On the contrary, she doesn't take on enough. Bolderton sees to that.'

'I'm talking about Alice.'

'The children's Alice?'

'Who else?'

We weren't talking about her.'

'I was.'

'If you try to carry on a conversation we haven't been having, you must expect to be misunderstood.'

Irving spoke with asperity. He had just found a red rose hidden in his pyjama trousers. A thorn had scratched him on the inner tender part of his thigh. It could have been worse – the flower was wedged in the crotch of his trousers. It was a totally risible situation. He mustn't give Helen the chance to use it. He had noted a certain wryness in her smile and knew enough psychology to foresee that she might be sufficiently piqued to tell it as an after-dinner story.

He threw the rose under the bed, making a mental note to remove it in the morning. He could not think of a way of rebuking the girl without making himself look absurd.

'What has Alice taken on?'

'I don't altogether trust her. She's two-faced.'

Irving, checking his pyjama trousers for thorns, said vexedly, 'I don't find her even one-faced – she's totally forgettable.'

'I suppose it follows.'

'What follows what?'

'One or two faces or none. She plans to be an actress.'

'Oh lord.'

'She's working to pay for her training at RADA. I daresay she practises.'

'Practises?'

'Registering emotion.' Helen said gravely, 'Perhaps she practises on you.'

Next morning when Irving looked under the bed, the rose had gone.

It was his turn to walk the children. He took them to the common. They ran screeching towards the ponds and he settled himself on a wooden seat with a view of the Surrey hills.

Midgeley and Alice were mingled in his thoughts. It was a matter of contemporaneity. In all else, of course, they were poles apart, except perhaps in ardour. One might say they were both desirous, Midgeley of an open-and-shut theory, Alice of some fanciful but fleshly consummation . . .

At that point Irving was obliged to get up and supervise his children who were making mud pies with their gloves on.

There were some fraught moments before he could take up his thoughts again, and then his thoughts took *him* up, by the scruff. He was vividly reminded of the last time he saw Midgeley.

Midgeley had sent for him, being by then confined to his bed. Irving found him still working, prematurely buried under books and papers. He was in a highly emotive state, exultant, frenetic and fearfully anxious. He babbled about a concept, not new – according to him it was as old as time and had been lying around under men's noses waiting to be noticed. Midgeley, it was obvious, believed that he was the unveiler of a universally important fact. It would, he said, 'equate the world'. Those were his words, but having spoken them, he was seized with feverish secrecy and scrambled all his papers out of sight under the bedclothes.

Irving, who was unaccustomed to illness, was surprised at the change in this unremarkable man. There was a weird brilliance about him, an apostolic fervour. Irving was irreligious and found it quite unsettling.

Midgeley planned to deliver his theory to the world as a Cardew lecture, forgetting or overlooking the fact that he hadn't been asked to speak. In the event of his indisposition preventing him from speaking, he wished to make Irving his executor. Irving would have been willing, had there been anything to execute. He had questioned Midgeley patiently until Midgeley had some sort of seizure and Irving had to leave. Next day Midgeley died. His paper was delivered to Irving by special messenger.

Irving had studied it with curiosity and increasing dismay. It was a mish-mash of science, theology and cloud-cuckoo. Midgeley's proposition, if it could be so called, was that good and evil exist in equal doles, issued to mankind for general consumption. Like two pieces of soap, thought Irving incredulously, soluble like soap – the implication being that in due time the supply would be used up and since good and evil could only exist in relation to each other there would be no occasion for sin and Man would return to his first state of innocence. There was some quasi-religious affiliation with a nuclear apocalypse – a sort of Big Wash, perhaps, to dispose of all the soap in one go.

Irving's pity was tinged with envy. Midgeley had found his Answer and, so to speak, gone off with it. Whether it was valid or not was immaterial.

There were times when Irving thought that the equation would never come out anyway. Let x equal a, equal z, equal any old thing, the quantities weren't merely unknown, they were incompatible.

But he got a shock, an unpleasant twinge, when he went into his study after lunch and found Midgeley's paper on his desk. Set fair and square in the centre, the damn silly title – 'Return to Eden' – scrawled across the front page.

Irving had locked it away in the bottom drawer. The drawer was still locked and the key on his key-ring. His own lecture notes, which he had left on his typewriter, had vanished.

Helen, as might be expected, knew nothing about it. He asked her, simply to ratify a doubt more than anything else. He *must* be mistaken and needed to hear her say so.

'You put the wrong ones away,' she said obligingly. 'It's easily done, one heap of paper looks much like another.'

'Not when one is in Midgeley's handwriting.'

'You've been working on it, haven't you?'

'Why should I be?'

'Aren't you going to read it at the Cardew?'

'Only if I want to make a laughing-stock of myself and of the faculty.'

'I thought he was your friend.'

'He was. But if I tell you that he was trying to apply the quantum theory to infinities – '

'I should be no wiser.'

'It's *my* paper I'm concerned about!'

'Don't shout.'

'Where is it?'

'I have no idea.'

'For God's sake! I'm due to read it this evening – '

He ransacked his study. Panicking, he ran downstairs and went through his overcoat. He turned out the pocket linings, opened and shook the umbrellas in the hallstand, flung everything off the hooks, including the children's coats. The children . . . He was snatching at straws. Reasoning would come later, if at all.

In the nursery he surprised a scene of simple charm. Caspar and Candida were kneeling at Alice's feet and she was reading them a story. She paused at the sight of Irving. The children gave him one glance and clamoured for her to go on.

She smiled dreamily at Irving. 'When the prince came to where Beauty lay sleeping, he placed a single red rose on her bosom and stooped to wake her with a kiss – '

'Not that!' cried Caspar. 'Tell about the gingerbread house.'

'Gingerbread – ugh!' said Candida. 'It was a coffee fudge house with a lemon meringue roof – I'd eat that first.'

'You couldn't reach the roof!'

'Naturally it was a little tiny house – '

'Have either of you been into my study?' said Irving.

Caspar shook his head. Candida, who overworked a word once she had learned it, said 'Naturally not.'

Irving looked at Alice. 'You – what about you?' She blinked those ridiculous eyelashes of hers, like spent matchsticks. 'Have you been into my study for any reason? Any reason at all?' She continued to gaze at him, though with what in mind he couldn't tell. 'Or for no reason? I want the truth!'

The children were wishing him to go away. Candida actually attempted to dismiss him. 'The witch put Hansel in a cage and poked him to see if he was fat enough for the oven – '

'Listen to me!' Irving, standing over them, spoke through his teeth. 'Some very important papers have disappeared from my study. I left them on top of the typewriter. If you know anything about them and own up now, I won't be angry. I won't punish you.'

It flashed on him then that a-morality could be what Alice and Midgeley had in common. It was, after all, the logical outcome of Midgeley's theory – a world without sin or virtue, and Alice's face, when one came to study it, as he was now, was not innocent, so much as uncommitted.

He felt that he was the victim of some sort of ridiculous conspiracy. He shouted over their heads, to the conspirator, 'Where the hell are my notes!'

Candida, who was bored, started a howl of convenience, the ploy of hers which invariably paid off. She could work up the decibels as confidently as any professional soprano.

'Candida, stop that noise!'

Helen had come into the room. She carried a sheaf of papers which she thrust at Irving. 'Is this what you're looking for?'

'My notes!'

'They've been flying around the kitchen.'

'Flying?'

'Like birds.'

Irving leafed through the sheets. They were out of order, but complete. 'If this is a joke, I hope it's over.'

'I hope so. And done with.'

'That's for me to say.'

'Meaning?'

84

'It was stupid and inconsiderate.' Irving's voice rose. 'It was a bloody fool thing – '

'Not in front of the children, please.' Helen turned and went.

Irving ran downstairs after her. 'Have you any idea of the work I put into this?'

In the kitchen she faced him. She was white and very tense.

'You told me it was a rehash of one of your course lectures.'

'That's still a hell of a lot of work. Am I to understand you took it to wrap the potato peelings?'

'I promise you I never laid a finger on your notes until they ended up at my feet.'

Irving smiled unpleasantly. 'Having flown in through the window? I think you said they were flying.'

Helen groped for a chair and sat down. 'I came into the kitchen and there they were. I thought that a lot of birds had got in – '

'Birds?'

'They were like seagulls – circling.'

'Are we talking about the same thing?'

'Sheets of paper flying round and round. So quiet – stealthy – horrid!'

She was genuinely upset. Irving said crisply, 'The effect of some sort of updraught. A current of air.'

'The windows were shut. There was no air!'

'The question is, how did my notes get out of my study and into the kitchen?'

'I don't know!'

'They flew in, of course!'

They stared at each other. Irving had no difficulty identifying Helen's thoughts. She knew she was being absurd and she was angry with herself, and with him for being unsympathetic. He took her hand.

She snatched it away. 'There's something else – ' She pointed across the room.

In a far corner, lying on its side on the floor, was a huge earthenware crock. It was unbroken, but the bags of flour that had been in it had burst, scattering their contents over a wide radius.

'What happened?'

'It missed me by inches,' said Helen.

'You hadn't put it securely on the shelf – '

'It flew at me!'

'*Flew*?'

'I could have been killed!'

'My dear, you have had a couple of minor but annoying accidents – '

'It flew off the shelf and didn't break!'

'It will certainly have cracked, but I agree it appears whole *in situ* – '

Irving approached the crock. Before he reached it, it started to roll gently to and fro.

Helen gasped. Irving hesitated. The thing was plainly unbroken and appeared to be demonstrating the fact. He seized it by its neck and set it upright. 'Vibration.'

'What vibration?'

'Possibly from the M 20.'

'The M 20 is miles away.'

'Or the fridge or the freezer.'

They stood listening. The kitchen, usually cosy with the working hum of domestic appliances, was stolidly silent. 'You see?' said Irving. 'It's really nothing.'

'Where are the birds?' Candida appeared in the doorway.

'Birds?'

'You said there were birds in the kitchen. I want to see them.'

'There are no birds.'

'You said!'

'It was a figure of speech,' said Helen.

Candida glared. 'Why do you say there are things if there aren't?'

Irving told Helen, 'I leave you to answer that one,' and went to his study. Midgeley's paper still reposed on his desk. He took it up and leafed through page after page of Midgeley's execrable handwriting. He secured it with a bulldog clip and put it in the bottom drawer of his desk. He had difficulty locking the drawer, somehow the key had become slightly bent.

He was spreading out his own notes and was starting to reassemble them in numerical order when he heard a scream followed by a rumble as of shifting heavy furniture.

As he ran into the hall, Helen came from the kitchen. Her eyes were wild, she had Candida by the shoulders, pushing the child before her.

'What is it? What's wrong?'

Helen could not speak, she was sobbing in her throat. Irving tried to touch her, she fought him off.

'For Heaven's sake – '

She spread her arms about the child, shielding her – Helen, his wife, shielding his child from him.

'Tell me what's happening!'

'The knife – '

'What knife?'

'The carving knife – it came straight at Candida!'

'Came?'

'Out of the air!'

Irving's heart sank. He was up against something which could not be wished away. Something in Helen, his calm, temperate, rational wife.

'Come, let's go and sit down. I'll get you something to drink – '

'It's there I tell you! Sticking in the table!'

He went into the kitchen, came back, trying to smile. 'There's nothing.'

'But the knife – '

'Is in the dresser drawer. Where it always is.'

'The table – '

'Is unmarked.'

'The table moved – came after us!'

'My dear – '

'Can I do anything?'

Alice and Caspar had come downstairs, Alice holding Caspar's hand. Helen cried out like an animal and snatched Caspar away.

'Just a small mishap,' said Irving.

'Small mishap?' My children's lives are in danger!'

'Candida,' Irving stooped to look into his daughter's eyes, 'what did you see?'

'I didn't see the birds.'

'Did you see anything?'

'I didn't!' Candida stamped her foot.

Caspar started to whimper. Irving said to Alice, 'Take them upstairs.'

Helen, very white, held both her children to her. 'They are never to go near that girl again.'

'Helen!'

'I'm taking them away and I shan't bring them back until she's out of the house!'

'What has Alice to do with it?'

'Everything!'

'For Heaven's sake, pull yourself together!'

Helen could be seen making the effort. Icy, but unsteady, she said, 'It's well known that this sort of thing can happen with adolescents.'

'What sort of thing?'

'Manifestations.'

'My dear – ' Irving swallowed. A little pseudo-science was harder to take than sheer vagary. 'That's mere supposition. Nothing's been proved, or can be proved – '

'It's not safe for any of us. You too,' said Helen, bundling the children into their coats, 'should be warned. Get her out of the house tonight. I'm going to my parents.'

'To Winchester?'

'I'll ring you tomorrow to check that she's gone.'

'You haven't packed – This is sheer folly!'

'I have my car-keys and enough petrol to get us there. That's all that matters.' Helen threw her own coat over her shoulders. 'I won't risk another moment here.'

She didn't. The next moment they were gone. Gusts of rain blew in through the open front door. Irving stood waiting for the sound of Helen's car. He made no move to stop them. He knew that Helen right or Helen wrong, it was best to let them go.

Alice, of course, had heard it all. He sighed, so did she, though without regret. She was merely taking in air. Her bosom rose, replenished.

'I'm sorry,' he said. 'My wife is rather upset.'

'It wasn't me.'

'You mustn't blame yourself.'

She moved to close the door. 'I don't have to go, do I?'

'I'm afraid you do. Helen – You see, something happened which she associates with you.'

'Why?'

'There's a belief – a superstition – that certain happenings – disturbances – are activated by the physical presence of someone your age. Someone who is growing up.' He was choosing his words. 'It's considered to be a difficult time.'

'I'd have felt something, wouldn't I?'

'I don't know.'

'Why couldn't it be her?' She could be having a difficult time.'

It was a distinct possibility – the only one, so far as he could see.

Helen was approaching the other difficult age of woman, the change of life – and sometimes of personality.

'I think you must go and pack your things.'

Alice sighed, this time with regret. 'I like it here.'

'I'm sorry.'

'Will you come and see me on the stage? I'm going to be an actress.'

'I know.'

'I'm going to be famous.' She sighed again, as if it would be a chore. 'I'll do all the big parts, St Joan, Rebecca, Hedda Gabler.'

Irving thought how provident she was being by despising what she hadn't got and might never get. Insuring against failure. He knew now what the matchstick eyelashes were the beginning of: make-up. She would need layers of it to make her up to St Joan, Rebecca, Hedda Gabler.

Then she said, 'The evil that men do lives after them, the good is often buried with their bones.'

'What?'

'It's Shakespeare.'

'But why say it?'

'Why not? I know lots of Shakespeare.'

It was Irving's turn to gaze. She had just shot a cherished proposition to pieces. The words made nonsense of Midgeley's paper. If they were to be believed, mankind was damned.

But Midgeley's paper was nonsensical anyway, and Irving certainly had not cherished it. He said, smiling, 'Shakespeare could be wrong, you know.' In a face as young as hers it was possible to see into every pore without distaste. He touched her cheek. 'This too, too solid flesh does melt.'

The Cardew lecture that evening was being moderately well attended. Hopcraft, as chairman, spoke briefly, acknowledging that Irving needed no introduction. Irving mounted the platform to a rustle of applause.

He plunged both hands in his pockets and stooped chummily towards his audience. 'This isn't the first time I've had the honour to contribute to this series of lectures. It's still a great and memorable occasion for me. Tonight I want to speak about the proliferation principle. I hope you may find something in my talk worth remembering – '

He hoped he wasn't smirking. He spread his notes on the lectern, glanced down at them. Glanced up, and down again. His smile fading, he gripped the lectern for support. He was seen to snatch up the sheets one by one, and one by one let them fall.

Hopcraft, on the platform with him, saw nothing amiss. The pages were neatly typed. On one which had fluttered down by his feet, he noted the title, 'Return to Eden'. It suffered from a dropped lower-case 'e', a peculiarity of Irving's machine.

THE PARROT

'AN EYE FOR an eye,' said the man who sat in the corner of the bar.

I said, talking about Ireland, 'These people are poking out their own.'

'An eye for an eye if the Lord requires it. In the matter of the Ark of the Covenant he was very fussy about the way it was made – I often wonder how Moses remembered everything. He had no shorthand. Of course he was up the Mount forty days and nights, time enough to memorise it. But there are eyes and eyes. If the eye of a needle rates the eye of a potato and the eye of a beast rates the eye of another beast, the eye of man shouldn't go for less.'

I went to get a beer, and when I returned he leaned out of his corner.

'The Bible's full of double talk. Look at my friend Billy Bligh, a man unlike other men, and went for next to nothing.'

We were knee to knee and I could see he wasn't going to talk about Ireland, I recognised the appetite of the teller for his tale.

'He had a workshop behind the old Alhambra, he was a toymaker, known in the trade as a craftsman and perfectionist. His regiments of wooden soldiers were accurate in every detail. You could count the bullets in their belts. He *built* his dolls' houses, every one different, modelled on a real house; if he knew the child it was going to, he modelled it on the child's own home. His houses had lights that lit and bells that rang. He even installed a little tank so that real water

91

came out of the taps. He was so clever with his hands he could cut the Lord's Prayer on an apple pip.'

I had heard that one before, and was about to counter with the story of the man who could get the Koran on a mustard-seed, but when I opened my lips he held up his hand like a policeman on traffic duty.

'Billy was an artist. That's why he never made any money. He barely charged enough to cover the cost of his materials. It was the work he cared about, not what he got for it. He never married, and he used to go every evening to a pub called the May Garland, in Commercial Road. It was pulled down long ago. In his day it was a cosy little place with plenty of brass and plush to cheer the eye and warm the fundament. Billy would sit in a corner and make his solitary pint last the evening. He didn't talk, he was a man of few words, just a smile and a nod when he went in, and the same when he went out.

'Nobody noticed him much. He was one of those people who aren't missed till they've been gone a month. And in the May Garland there was no lack of talkers. Even if everyone in the public was to fall silent there was one ready to fill the pause. An African parrot.

'The landlord had been a sailor and he brought it home with him from his last voyage and put a ring on its leg and chained it to a perch behind the bar. It had picked up quite a repertory from its spell at sea, it was a quick learner, and plenty of people were ready to teach it. While Billy Bligh sat never uttering a word, that bird talked, sang, whistled, barked, cat-called, cried like a baby and made a noise like a turnstile. It used the salt blue language you'd expect from the lower decks. When it hung upside down, blinking its yellow eye, or put its head on one side and just stared, you could swear it had your measure. It was the life, if not the soul, of the May Garland. When it was in the mood it could keep the place in a roar. Billy used to smile and nod at the bird as if it was human. It gave him an idea for a toy, a wooden parrot that spun round and round on its perch. He made several.

'Then one day there came a new barmaid, a girl with a face like an angel. She didn't just hand Billy his beer and take his money, she smiled and wished him a good evening. Her name was Phoebe – the moon goddess, and that's what she seemed to Billy.

'It was love at first sight. For someone who had never felt anything of the sort, it was a shattering experience. He came away from the bar counter with his head in a whirl and his beer running over. He sat in his corner and watched her, didn't take his eyes off her the whole evening. He put down three pints instead of his usual one, for the pleasure, the sheer heart-stopping thrill of her look and smile and kindly word when he went to the bar to order.

'It was clear that she was going to be a treasure. The men in the May Garland started to treasure her, in their various ways, from the very first beer she served, drawing the china beer-pull so firmly and tenderly to her bosom. What wouldn't they give – they said openly – to be that lucky beer handle.

'For the first time in his life Billy wanted to talk, words seethed in his head, sweet private words. But when he put down his empty tankard and she turned and looked into his eyes, the ground opened under his feet. All he could say was, "The same again, Miss." The parrot, which had been tipping silently over and over on its perch, bawled, "Look the other way, dear, I'm shy!" Everybody laughed. Phoebe smiled, and when she passed his beer she gently touched Billy's hand.

'He went back to his corner. He made up his mind he would do better. He must work out something to say to her, that he could actually say and be heard to say – private words would come later. But nothing that other people might hear seemed worth saying. The commonplace, even the common language, had no place with her.

'When he went for his third pint he trod lightly because he had already drunk twice as much as usual. Tom Dooley, a coal heaver, was at the bar monopolising her attention. Billy did not mind waiting, for he could watch the little pearl bones at the base of her throat. They reminded him of the inlays he put on his musical boxes. But mother-of-pearl did not move him nearly to tears as those little knuckle bones in her slender neck did.

' "Put your tongue in!" screeched the parrot in his ear, and went into ribald cackles. "You're making a puddle."

'Dooley gave Billy a nudge which sent him staggering. "You can keep the parrot, mate, I'll take the bird."

' "Another pint please," Billy said, to hide his embarrassment. The girl gave him a smile which sent arrows into his heart. The parrot shouted, "Try a rum in your beer, dear!" Everyone chuckled, and Billy went back to his corner and did not try again to speak to Phoebe that evening.

'But he dreamed about her all night, and next day he had no joy in his work. When he looked at the rocking horse he was carving he found that he had chiselled off the ears and gouged out the eyes and ruined the head. So he put it away and gave himself up to thinking about Phoebe.

'He had no experience with women, how to handle them or what to make of them: it was news to him that there was making to be done. Without being any way abnormal he had found all his pleasure and satisfaction in his toys: you could call him unawakened. But like Beauty, Sleeping Billy, once his eyes were opened, meant to make up for lost time.

'His instinct was right. That evening he took the girl a present, an elephant carved out of an orange pip.'

'An orange pip?' I was wondering what he'd done about the trunk.

'An orange pip. For her luck, and his. He went early, but news of Phoebe's charms had travelled fast and the bar was already half full. Dooley was buying drinks for everyone because it was his birthday. Billy didn't get the chance of asking her for his pint, it was called and paid for by Dooley.

'He sat down to wait. He wasn't feeling patient: he had the elephant in his fist and some choice words on his lips, chosen for her. There she was, behind the bar, the sweet and pretty girl, his intended. Oh he intended! There was no other way to settle his stomach.

'The parrot was hunched on its perch. It had been used to holding the floor, people hanging on its words, ready to laugh if it so much as scratched itself. Now they were hanging on the smiles of the girl and it's my belief the bird was jealous.

'Dooley and his cronies were having a bit of a party. They were gathered at one end of the bar and Billy saw his opportunity when Dooley, who was drunk, turned away to put whisky into the parrot's drinking water. Billy went up to Phoebe and took her hand. He dropped the elephant into her palm – "It's a present." She was startled, it turned out she was short-sighted, she could hardly see the thing. "It's lovely," she said, peering, "what is it?" "It's a lucky charm," said Billy, "you know, like a black cat." "But it's not black." "No, it's white, a white elephant." "And will it bring me luck?" "Yes, if you keep it with you always." "Oh, I shall," she said, "I can do with some luck." Billy held on to her hand. "There's something I want to tell you."

'He was going to tell her he loved her – in his innocence he thought to get it settled then and there. But before he could speak, the parrot bawled, "Take your corsets off and let's have fun!"

'It was the end of chosen words. Phoebe blushed and turned away. The parrot had everyone's attention, it rocked on its perch and bawled the naval ratings' lament – "I heard the voice of Moses say – roll on my bloody twelve!"

'Billy went away to his corner. He had always been a mild man: only his mother, long dead, would have recalled the paddy he had on him as a baby. It was rising now, but now it was a man's paddy, with more to it than kicking heels and screaming. He sat a long time watching Phoebe, waiting for another chance. Dooley kept her busy, setting up rounds for his friends, and, as he became drunker and maudlin, treating his enemies as well. Finally, he went down as if he had been poleaxed: Phoebe leaned her elbows on the bar and laughed to see them struggle to lift the man like his own coal sacks. It was Billy's chance to get her to himself.

' "I'll wait for you and walk you home tonight," he said. "I don't go home," she said, "I'm living in." "But I must talk to you – " "You're doing that, aren't you?" She looked at him, serious, not pert, and he began to suspect that there was a bit of a game to be played – and he was one down already. "It's private," he said, "for your ears alone." "No one will hear," she said softly, and leaned across the bar so that her two shy pretty bosoms came close to his hand.

'Billy's head began to spin. He tried to speak, but his wits blew away like sparks. He managed to whisper, "I love you," but it was lost, shot down, you might say, in a blood-splitting screech from the parrot. That bird was eaten up with jealousy.

'Billy lost his nerve. As I said, he was innocent, a child where women were concerned, and like a child, dismayed and angry, he yelled, and because she hadn't heard what he believed was going to change the world, he yelled it. "I love you!"

'That was his undoing, the whole lovely bundle fell to bits. The parrot, which had a throat like brass, took it up and broadcast it right through the public, the saloon and the snug – "I love you!" – turning over and over on its perch like a split pin in a wagon wheel. "I love you, I love you, I love you!"

'Everyone slapped everyone else and joked, and capped their jokes, and fell about laughing. Billy wasn't a mixer, never one of the boys, and they enjoyed seeing him taken down a peg. Every face was split from ear to ear – he wouldn't have cared a straw if the girl hadn't been laughing too.

'There and then he made up his mind. He waited in his corner for them to forget about him. Which they soon did, and when it was time for last calls, he slipped into the lavatory. He stayed there until the bar was empty. Dooley had been carried out, Phoebe had covered the beer engine and doused the lights and gone up to her room. There was no sound except the rattle of the parrot's chain as it sidled to and fro on its perch. Billy came out, groped his way silently to the bar counter, took up the bird and wrung its neck.

'He didn't get off scot free, he was bitten on the hand. The stickiness of his blood and the shock of what he had done made him feel faint. To revive himself he took a swig of whisky from the bar. As his eyes got used to the dark, he saw the body of the bird dangling by one foot on the end of its chain. "Nothing to shout about?" he said, and wrapping his hand in his sleeve pulled back the bolts and went home.

'His anger, slow to rouse, was soon over. He had no regrets, and he wasn't the man to feel pleased with himself. He was reasonably satisfied that he had done what needed to be done, and now there would be nothing to keep him from speaking to the girl, or her from listening.

'The wound on his hand did not trouble him, he bandaged it as best he could. Afterwards he went to bed and slept serenely as a baby.

'Next day he worked at his swinging parrots. They were a good line, he had had repeat orders. It's an ill wind, and he painted them the same colours as the parrot in the bar, grey with scarlet tail feathers. RIP, he thought, and hung each one up by its foot to dry. After that he didn't give it another thought. That evening he did as he always did on entering the May Garland, he looked for Phoebe. He wasn't a fanciful or romantic nature, but he had killed a bit of a dragon for her.'

'Dragon?' I said.

'Dragon,' the man in the corner insisted. 'There she was, the sweet and pretty girl, his intended, and he went straight up to her, a free and honourable man, to declare himself. She had seen him come in and as she drew his beer she cried, "Who could have done it? Someone's wrung poor Joey's neck!"

' "If I catch whoever did it, I'll wring his!" vowed Dooley. An angry murmur went round the bar.

' "I came in here this morning," said Phoebe, "and found him hanging by his foot. It was horrible. I'll never forget it."

' "That bird was human," said Dooley.

' "This place won't be the same without it."

' "There was blood all over the bar," said Phoebe. "Joey bit whoever killed him."

' "Who could do a thing like that!"

97

' "I couldn't fancy a man that was cruel to animals," said Phoebe.

' "I loved that bird," said Dooley.

' "A man that could do that could do other things." said Phoebe. "Other things?" said Billy. "He could kill a child, or an old woman," said Phoebe. "It wasn't a child or an old woman," said Billy, and tried to take her hand. She picked up a cloth and wiped the bar counter. "A man like that could do a murder." "It wasn't a murder," said Billy, "it was a nuisance, the riddance of a nuisance." She stopped wiping the counter and stared at him. "Why do you say that?" When he reached out to touch her, she cried, "What have you done to your hand?"

' "Let's see," said Dooley.

' "It's just a scratch," said Billy, putting his hand in his pocket.

'Dooley stepped up to him, "Show me your hand."

' "Show me your hand," said Billy. Dooley pushed his fist into Billy's face. "There's mine, it's not scratched and it's not bitten." Behind Billy's back, people started to murmur.

' "He said Joey was a nuisance."

' "Good riddance, he said."

' "He was here last night."

' "When did he leave?"

' "I never saw the going of him," said Phoebe.

'Dooley pushed Billy up against the bar. Billy struggled, but Dooley was a big man, he held Billy by the slack of his waistcoat and dragged Billy's hand out of his pocket. They all saw the bandage, heavily stained with blood.

' "It was him!"

' "Bligh killed Joey!"

' "Oh," cried Phoebe, "he would never do a wicked cruel thing like that!"

'Dooley hoisted Billy's bandaged hand in front of them like a flag. They were all looking at him, they had never particularly liked him, whatever he said, they wouldn't believe, they would hold it against him. But he knew what he had better *not* say. The murmurs were getting louder, like breakers that start far out and roll in and smash you on the beach.

' "You did it," said Dooley.

' "You did it," said Billy.

' "By God!" Dooley turned to his friends. "He's accusing me!"

'They came round, jostling Billy, men he saw every day in the May Garland. They looked different, ugly.

' "If you wrang that bird's neck, is there any reason why I shouldn't wrang yours?"

'They shouted, "Do it, Dooley! Give him a good hiding!" Someone threw his beer into Billy's face. "Speak up," Dooley said, shaking him, "it's your last chance."

'Billy put his head on one side. His tongue ran about his mouth like a mouse, but the words came out in a trumpet blast. "I heard the voice of Moses say – roll on my bloody twelve!"

'He had a split second to raise his own goose prickles, and then they came at him, every man jack with hand, or boot, or both, lifted against him.

'Billy wasn't a hero, or a martyr. With his good hand he punched Dooley in the groin and broke free.

'He dived through the crowd, using his head and his knees to split them. He was bent double when he burst out through the door of the May Garland into the street. No eyes in the top of his head, so he didn't see the Peckham tram careering down the hill. Broke the boom and brought down the wires he did – and died of a broken neck.'

The man got up out of his corner and went to the door.

'Goodnight, dear,' the barmaid called after him. 'See you in my dreams.'

'See you in my dreams.'

Everyone to his taste, I thought. She was a big blubber-lipped girl and I did not fancy her.

'Who was that?' I asked.

'Oh, he's not a bad old bird,' she said. 'We call him Mr. Polly.'

THE DOLL

IF I HAD liked my godfather more I might have disliked the doll less. I call him uncle Jack. He's not my uncle, I don't know what he is. I said to him 'I've got a father, I've got Daddy, and God's *the* Father, where do you come in?' 'I'm your fairy godfather,' he said, and my mother laughed.

He was always buying me things to eat, chocolates and toffees and marzipan mice. I overheard my mother say, 'You mustn't, Jack, the child's overweight as it is.' To me, she said, 'Too much sugar makes you bilious.' After that, he bought me the doll.

'Her name's Lilli Marlene,' he said. 'She's from Germany, where all the best dolls come from.'

Everyone said what a pretty doll she was, the first thing people said was what a very *pretty* doll. To me it wasn't a source for rejoicing. When my mother said 'It's just like him,' I knew she wasn't talking about the doll but about the quality of the gift. And the giver. She has a dreamy look when she talks about my godfather. They're not dreams I can share. To me, he *was* like the doll: he looks as if he's been made and not born. His skin is china-smooth, his hands small and manicured.

From the first I didn't know what to do with her. She's a lady doll. She wears a blue satin gown, low cut, she has bosoms moulded in white kid, a spreading skirt which just clears her tiny feet in buckled shoes. Her hair isn't real, it's gold thread. I can see the beads of glue where it's stuck to her head. She has a beauty-spot on one cheek but she doesn't have any knickers, her legs are china at the bottom and cloth at the top.

I couldn't undress her, she is stitched into her dress: I couldn't comb her hair and I wouldn't wheel her out in my dolls' pram because she doesn't go with my dear old Peter Rabbit and my baby doll which cries and wets its nappy when squeezed.

'I don't like her mouth,' I told my mother.

'Why not? It's a perfect mouth – a rosebud.' My mouth is square like a letterbox. From that moment I hated the doll.

I hated touching her. I put her in her box and hid her under my bed. My mother made me take her out. I was ungrateful, she said, there were little girls in the Third World didn't even have enough to eat. As this was said whenever I didn't finish my dinner I chose to ignore it, and took Lilli into the garden and left her under a bush.

That night I lay listening to the rain, thinking of her getting wetter and wetter, her satin dress going black and slimy like the things in the pond, her white and pink and gold running together, her hair sinking into the hole in her head, china dolls have holes in their heads. I thought she'll be a mess, they won't say she's pretty and I'll say I forgot her. I forgot Peter Rabbit once, it rained all night and he looked terrible and they wanted to put him in the dustbin. I wouldn't let them, I'd let them put her. But next day when I went to look, she was gone from under the bush. My mother found her sitting in the summer-house, her hands in her lap. 'How pretty she is,' my mother said.

Uncle Jack teased me, took the doll in his arms, danced with her cheek to cheek, singing a song about Lilli Marlene, lady of the lamplight. The doll laughed at me over his shoulder, opening her rosebud to reveal a little red tongue.

When my father saw her he said, 'Who's this?'

Lilli Marlene, I said, from Germany. He said yes, he had heard. I said what had he heard, he said she was a bit before his time. I said what did she *do*? He believed she'd been faithful, he said.

He makes pipes, big ones for under the ground and has to

go away to see they're properly buried. That's when Uncle Jack comes and stays because my mother doesn't like being alone.

'You're not alone,' I said, 'I'm here.'

'Darling, I must have a man about the house.' She ruffled my hair.

We go to the seaside in the summer. I like the seaside. It doesn't care, it's always so busy. Eating up the land's important. You can see how far it's got when the tide's out. The rocks are bitten down to stumps, every year it comes in closer. It wants to get to the soft sand which it will swallow whole.

My father doesn't come to the seaside. My godfather comes. 'I wish Daddy was coming,' I said, 'it's not the same without him.'

'August's a busy month for pipes.' Uncle Jack winked.

'Pack your toys,' said my mother. 'And don't forget Lilli.'

'I don't want to take her.'

'Why not?'

I knew why not. I also knew that I was alone in this, and in anything which concerned my mother and my godfather. Nothing personal, they just seem to stop recognising me. I said, 'She doesn't like the seaside, it makes her bilious.'

My mother was smiling but firm. 'Take Lilli with you or Uncle Jack will think you don't love her.'

'I don't. And he's not my uncle.'

'Darling, a godfather's a very special relationship.'

We stay in one of the bungalows overlooking the beach. It's called Seabrim. If I stand at the gate and half shut my eyes I see towers in the sky. My mother said that was Cloud Cuckooland. Uncle Jack said it was Africa. He pinched her cheek to make her smile.

I'm allowed to go to the beach by myself if I don't get out of sight of the house. I suppose they watch me, I don't know, I never see them watching.

My mother said, 'You mustn't stay indoors this lovely day, go to the beach and play.'

'There's no-one to play with.'

'Make a sandcastle, we'll come and look at it presently. And put on your sun-hat.'

I decided to take Peter Rabbit for company. The baby, Chuckles, I left asleep in his cot. Lilli I hadn't unpacked. I sat Peter in the pram with the canopy down so that he would get a good view, he only has one eye. I went indoors to fetch my hat and when I came out Lilli was sitting in the pram with the canopy up and Peter was upside down in the bottom.

My mother must have done it, though I wondered when she could have taken Lilli out of my suitcase. Certainly not while I was fetching my sunhat. Anyway, I didn't dare put Lilli out. 'Stuff you!' I said. She looked through me.

That first day on the beach I was lucky. I thought I was, I met Margie. She had stuck a bottle in the sand and was throwing pebbles at it and missing. She said, 'Hi,' I said 'Lo.' 'Let's use bigger stones' she said and we smashed the bottle. I worried about leaving broken glass where people came to paddle. Margie said she knew of a pool with crabs in. We went to look.

Margie wore a bright red swim-suit, she ran barefoot over the rocks while I was slipping and slithering on smelly sea-weed.

There was only one crab in the pool. We poked it. Margie picked it up by one of its legs and ran screaming down to the sea with it. I hoped it would swim away but she said it was dead or would be when the big fish got it.

She wanted us to go for a walk along the dunes. I said I'd have to fetch my pram. Pram, did I think she was going to push me? she said. My dolls' pram, I said.

She slapped her knees and shrieked with laughter. She was what my mother would call rough. I was beginning to feel a bit unsettled myself. She ran back over the rocks, I went up the beach and walked on the sand to where I had left the pram.

Margie was doing handstands which I'm not allowed to, my mother says it's indelicate for a girl. 'What's that?' Margie said, pointing to Peter.

'Obviously it's a rabbit,' I said.

She looked under the canopy where Lilli was sitting, shaded and cool, her little pricky hands in her lap, pretty as a picture. If you like that sort of picture.

'And what's *this*?'

I didn't say anything. Let her find out, I thought, let them both find out.

'Christ,' said Margie, 'I grew out of dollies years ago.' I went cold then hot. I've been brought up sheltered, but not so sheltered that I don't know swearing when I hear it. 'You're a booby, a big fat booby!' Her being thin and wiry as a spider, it went home. 'I wouldn't be seen dead in that hat, I bet you've got frilly knickers!'

She did another handstand. From upside down she pretended to look under my skirt. I held my dress over my knees. 'I have not!'

She dropped to her feet, went to the pram and picked up Lilli. 'This thing's spooky. I wouldn't be seen dead with it.' Crying 'Catch!' she threw the doll to me. I was slow to move. 'Butterfingers!' Lilli had fallen on a stone. 'It's broken. Do you mind?'

I looked at the network of fine cracks all over the pink and white face and felt an overwhelming sense of relief. 'Why should I mind?'

Margie turned the doll upside down. 'It's got no knickers!'

I laughed for pure joy because suddenly Lilli Marlene was an *it*, a china and rag thing. We both laughed. Margie swung the thing by one of its legs, whirled it round and round her head. Laughter possessed us, we shrieked and staggered about, laughing.

Then the china leg tore away from the cloth, Margie was left with the leg in her hand, complete with buckled shoe. We stopped laughing. Sobered, we looked at the doll lying on the stones. Margie put out a bare foot and pushed it away. It was rolled over and over by a little wave.

I picked it up and threw it as far as I could out to sea. Margie dug in the sand and buried the china leg.

'Got to go now,' she said cheerfully. 'See you.'

I watched until her red swimsuit had disappeared among the dunes. I didn't want to see her again.

Of course I started to worry how I was going to explain the doll's disappearance. People can always tell when I'm lying. Thought of telling the truth made me go cold.

It was quiet back at the bungalow, the curtains were drawn over my mother's bedroom window. She rests in the afternoon. I sat on the gate swinging back and forth to make it creak and break the quiet which was ready and waiting to hear what I was going to say. I saw the towers of Africa on the horizon. I thought about lies, because that was one, but nobody minded Uncle Jack telling it.

When the man came, his feet chuff-chuffed on the sand as he ran. He was sweating so much he had to wipe his glasses before he could see me. He asked could he use our phone. I've been told never to let a stranger into the house on any pretext, so I said no.

'Is your mother about? Or your father? Is there anyone? It's an emergency. A little girl has broken her leg, I must ring for an ambulance.'

'What little girl?'

'I found her lying among the dunes, unconscious. But maybe you know her? She's wearing a red bathing suit.'

I said we didn't have a phone, which is true, we don't at the bungalow, and he went chuff-chuffing away to the next house.

My mother looks pretty when she's angry. It makes me want to cry, seeing her angry and pretty.

'I wish you wouldn't leave your toys in my room!'

'I didn't – '

'And what on earth have you been doing? Your face is covered in scratches and just look at your dress! Soaking wet!'

'The question is,' Uncle Jack wasn't smiling, he had his hands behind his back like a policeman, '*when* did you?'

105

'I didn't!' Confused and scared, I touched my dress. It was stained, water dripped from the hem.

'Answer me!' cried my mother. 'When did you come to my room?'

'Steady on, don't frighten the kid,' Uncle Jack said. 'The door was locked – wasn't it?'

'Of course! And the doll wasn't there when we – ' She bit off the next word.

'The doll?'

They looked at me the way they do, as if they don't recognise me. I burst into tears.

'We found this little lady sitting on the end of the bed, large as life and twice as pretty.' My godfather produced her from behind his back, pink and white and gold in her satin gown, her two tiny feet in buckled shoes. I could see the pointed red tongue lurking in her rosebud mouth.

FUR

WHEN GLENDA MARRIED Bertram Lacey she didn't dream she would be marrying his Great-Aunt Selene too. Bertram saw fit to mention the old lady's existence only after they had been married a month, and Glenda thought it meant that their honeymoon had put everything else out of his mind, and Selene wouldn't figure much in their lives anyway. She was wrong on both counts.

'Selene? Isn't that something to do with the moon?'

'Something, yes,' said Bertram.

'What sort of thing?'

'Selene's the moon goddess.'

'Okay, so is Great-Auntie changeable? Fickle? Silvery?' Glenda smiled, but she was probing.

'You'll see.'

Glenda did. Great-Auntie turned up, uninvited, one Saturday just as they were setting out for lunch at their preferred pub.

'This is Selene,' said Bertram, stooping from his height to embrace what Glenda saw, at first, as an unassisted fur coat. The wearer had to be looked for. Looking, Glenda discovered a tiny face, pink and white and pretty as a doll's. It was topped by a chronically green scarf. (She never did find out if Great-Aunt had any hair, a scarf of some totally unsuitable colour was always swathed round her head.)

'Selene, this is Glenda,' said Bertram.

The little creature put out a hand, and taking it, Glenda was aware of a sensation in her arm, a sort of sparking, neither pleasant nor unpleasant.

107

'Hi, it's good to know you,' said Glenda, putting heart into it.

'She's American!' Selene told Bertram.

'We met in Washington,' he said.

'At the Lincoln Memorial,' added Glenda. 'I lived in Washington. I've been inside the Memorial lots of times. Guess I know the Gettysburg thing by heart. But that day it was brewing up a storm.'

'Washington rain,' said Bertram, 'you don't wait for.'

'I hadn't taken an umbrella. If I had, I wouldn't have met Bertie.' Glenda realised she was talking unnecessarily. It was because of Selene's merry eyes, she couldn't think what there was to be so merry about. 'It's a shame you didn't let us know you were coming, we're going out to lunch.'

'To The Bear,' said Bertram. 'Why don't you come, Auntie?'

'It's a pub,' Glenda said hastily. 'I'm sure your great-aunt – '

'I love bears,' said Selene. To Glenda she said, 'You killed them.'

'I beg your pardon?'

'There aren't any bears in America. You killed them all.'

'That's not true. Of course we have bears – '

Bertram laughed, laughing at Glenda.

The Bear was crowded, as always Saturday lunchtime. They started to go up to the Snug where there were window seats, but Selene teetered on the stairs and space was made for them at a table in the saloon.

'Will it be your usual, Auntie?' said Bertram. 'Gin and tonic?'

When he had gone for the drinks Selene sat twinkling at Glenda with a pleasure which, somehow, was not for sharing. That was in itself displeasing, but the real source of Glenda's displeasure was the fur coat sitting right beside her. She couldn't help looking into its roots, felt an obligation to do so. The hair was blackish brown and coarse, with none of the gloss of a properly treated skin. Shaggy was the word for it, and smelly, like the smell of old books, musty yet rank. Glenda recalled getting whiffs of the same at the zoo.

'Won't you take your coat off? It's warm in here.' For answer Selene retreated farther, if that were possible, into the depths of the fur.

Bertram brought two lagers and a gin and tonic. Selene's small face fairly shone. 'You remembered the cherry!' She took it up on its stick and gave, Glenda thought, a good imitation of a mouse nibbling. Then she drank the gin.

While Glenda and Bertram lunched on country paté and French bread, Selene chose game pie and chips. She was, she said, vegetarian in principle but didn't like to be a nuisance when she was asked out.

'What kind of fur is your coat?' said Glenda.

'Bear.'

'Bear fur?'

Selene speared a chip on her fork and nibbled it with the same enjoyment as she had the cherry. 'It was a dancing bear.'

'Now Auntie,' Bertram winked at Glenda, 'don't be naughty.'

'I'd like another gin, dear,' said Selene. 'A pink one this time.'

'A-t'elle une tête faible?' Glenda asked Bertram.

Selene said, 'No, I have a strong head.'

Bertram, grinning, went away to the bar. 'Is there some special reason why you won't take your coat off?' Glenda said.

'I feel safer with it on.' When Bertram brought the pink gin she exclaimed with joy. 'Oh, how pretty!'

'It had better be the last,' Glenda said under her breath.

Selene asked for and was served with chocolate pudding and caramel fudge sauce. Then Bertram took her home, and that took care of their cherished Saturday afternoon. Glenda asked where Selene lived. Bertram said in Bermondsey, in happy squalor.

'I want to know about that fur,' said Glenda. 'There's raccoon and muskrat and silver fox and mink and I've seen sable on your Royals, but I only ever saw fur like that walking on its own four legs. Where did she get it?'

'She feels the cold,' was all Bertram would say.

One week later Selene arrived, still wearing the coat and bearing a bunch of anemones, a flower that Glenda disliked. On the doorstep she shyly proffered them. 'You don't see flowers in your country, it's all skyscrapers and els.'

'Els?'

'Overhead railways. There's no room on the ground.'

Glenda cried 'Of course there is – of course we have flowers!' She sounded absurd, but was too vexed to care.

'Oh dear.' Selene seemed to shrink, she retreated down the steps, the anemones dropping from her hand. 'I'm so sorry – '

'Wait!' Finding herself addressing the coat, which was about all she could see, Glenda sounded peremptory. 'Don't go!' A breeze blew from off the fur directly into her nose. She caught a concentrated whiff of zoo and mouldy books. She sneezed. 'You'll have to leave that coat outside.'

'My coat?'

The thing could be full of fleas, thought Glenda. She had read that after feeding they could live for weeks without further sustenance. 'Leave it here in the porch.'

'Here?'

'I can't have it in the house.'

'Why not?'

'I'm allergic to fur.' Glenda said, 'It gives me asthma,' which was less hurtful than the truth and by way of being a white lie.

'Oh dear!' Selene's face crumpled with dismay. 'I'd better not come in – '

'Of course you must come in! Take off your coat, put it here beside the rubber-tree.'

'Someone might – '

'No-one will. And you won't be cold, I promise. We'll turn on the central heating.'

Divested of the coat, Selene showed herself a wisp of a creature. Glenda wondered how she sustained the weight of the coat – or managed to stay on the ground without it.

They sat in the kitchen, had coffee and dipped into the cookie-jar. The conversation centred round the difference between the English biscuit and the American cookie. Glenda said a cookie was more of a sweet cake. But 'bis' of course was French for twice, and 'cuit' for cooked. Selene cried 'Well I never!' and Glenda gave her a searching look. 'It's pretty obvious if you speak French.' Selene flinched. She had real talent for making herself smaller than she already was. Glenda saw why Bertram was concerned for her. It will make two of us, she thought. 'Shall you mind if I call you Auntie?'

Selene said she'd be honoured, and plainly meant it.

Glenda said, 'Anyone really nice we also call a cookie. Is it okay if I say something personal?'

'Oh – okay!' Selene said eagerly.

'That coat you wear – it doesn't do anything for you.'

'My fur? It does everything for me – '

'Where did it come from?'

'I found it outside my door, wet through, and took it in.'

'Took it in? It's not alive!'

'It was once. It was a bear, it danced.'

'How do you know?'

'I saw one in Spain. Or Italy, I can't remember which. It was a lovely dancer.'

'Honey, that fur coat just isn't you.'

Selene drew a breath, a deep one which increased her girth by about a millimetre. 'They say that after death our spirits return to earth in animals.'

Glenda laughed. 'I have no intention of coming back as a rabbit.'

'If I was allowed to choose, I'd choose to be big and strong, and able to take care of myself.'

'A bear?' Glenda teased. 'Do you believe everything you're told?'

Selene said sulkily, 'I don't believe a cookie's a person.'

All the late spring and summer she continued to come. Glenda never knew when. She would appear, in the coat, which she wore right through the warm weather, obediently taking it off before she entered the house and parking it in the porch with the rubber-plant. And Glenda, who had thought she was marrying Bertram, a marriageable man, found herself tied by bonds other than matrimony to a little old woman, self-effacing as a mouse. But much more prevalent.

It said a lot for both of them that she didn't mind. They sat in the kitchen where Selene liked best to be. It emerged that she was accustomed to being in one room, the sense of being which one room imparts; enclosure, if you like, safety if you prefer. Glenda preferred it. She realised that at Great-Aunt Selene's age, shrinkage was necessary. It was a matter of coping.

'Life,' Glenda said to Bertram, giving the word full weight, 'is just too much for her.'

'She seems to be doing alright. In her own way.'

'The way bothers me,' said Glenda. 'She's got an idea into her head that everything has its own spirit.'

'Spooks?'

'More like a battery that keeps a clock ticking.'

'Well, why not?'

'I do mean *everything*. Birds and beasts, plants and trees, sticks and stones.' Glenda laughed, a trifle wildly. 'Pots and pans!'

'Well, if it amuses her — '

'It bugs her! She worries she'll annoy something. She asked do I think grass dreads being cut.'

'She isn't the only one to think along those lines. It's called animism,' said Bertram.

'And does the percolator mind perking, for God's sake!' Glenda's laugh was definitely edgy. 'I've tried talking her out of it. She agrees it's crazy and goes away and comes right back and tells me she's scared to break an egg.'

'Darling,' Bertram was contrite, 'how deadly for you. I'll tell her she must snap out of it, it's getting you down.'

'Actually, it's become quite a game, guessing what all the spirits are like. A percolator, for instance: we ruled out cof-fee-colour because coffee's not integral to the machine, it's an addition, you could say an imposition. We figured the percolator's spirit would be meshy and pure white like on the day it was made, before the coffee got into its system and clogged up its pores. And what about the spirit of a spin-dryer?' Glenda said dreamily, 'A real little humdinger!'

'Don't look at me like that.'

'Like what?'

'Like you've been privatised!' cried Bertram. 'It's got to stop. I'll talk to her.'

Before he could do that, Great-Aunt Selene gassed herself trying to get a spark by rubbing two sticks together in order to avoid having to strike a match. She didn't die, just became more original, and retiring to the point of vanishment.

'We must do something or she'll fade out,' said Glenda, and arranged to have her taken into a home for senior citizens. 'You'll like it,' she told Selene. 'You won't have to break or strike or cut anything.' She did not say it will be done for you. The important thing was that Selene should not have to feel even remotely responsible.

'What about my fur?'

'You won't need that. It's lovely and warm at The Harbour and when you go out we'll take you in the car.'

There was pathetically little to dispose of after she left her room in Bermondsey. Glenda donned rubber gloves and took the coat to the municipal refuse dump.

Selene liked the home, and the senior citizens. Far from retiring, she came into her own, which was a surprise to everyone. Even to the Matron. 'I don't know where she gets it all,' she told Glenda, but would not, or could not go into detail.

Glenda and Bertram took a holiday. He became anxious after he found her in the garden with her fingers in her ears because he'd been knocking tacks into the stair-carpet. Watching her, he thought she was picking up things with caution, even timidity. She seemed to have lost her confidence with household chores. She was concentrating, he thought, quite beyond what she was doing, and certainly beyond him, on something which she couldn't share.

But after a fortnight in Bermuda she was so much more

herself that he fell in love with her all over again. They spent a rapturous second honeymoon, swimming, snorkelling, drinking rum punch and making love. They returned, suburnt and conspicuous, to a grey English winter. Glenda, who had thought of Great-Aunt Selene as she cracked the claws of a lobster, went at once to The Harbour to find out how she was. She met the Matron in the reception area and was told that Selene was quite well.

'You mean she's not as well as all that?' Glenda said anxiously.

'I mean *completely* well. Fully rigged, one might say,' said the Matron who had a nautical turn of phrase.

'No problems?'

'Not since she stopped walking round the house at night. She frightened some of our residents. It *was* quite frightening – she was wearing her fur coat and even I – '

'Fur coat?'

'A brownish black fur, it could have been well – anything in the dark.'

'She has no fur coat. I got rid of it when she came here.'

There was a pause. Then the Matron said brightly, 'Shall we go and look in her wardrobe? She's downstairs at the moment, having her tea.'

Selene's room, rigorously neat and ship-shape in accordance with the nursing-home standards, bore no visual signs of Selene. But there was a smell of mouldy books and beast in the air. Glenda sneezed.

'Bless you,' Matron said, and opened the wardrobe.

It was there, on a hanger, its fur bedraggled, matted and balled with mud. It looked sick, sick and tired.

Glenda's stomach turned. 'How did that get here?'

'Strange.' Matron touched it gingerly. 'It feels quite wet. But she can't have been out in the rain, the weather's been too squally to let them in the grounds.'

'Get rid of it.'

'Rid of what?'

'The coat!'

'Really – Are you sure? Is it what she would want?'

114

'It's what I want. The thing's unhygienic to say the least. It must be full of germs. Burn it.'

To Selene, Glenda was careful not to show surprise. 'You got your coat back then.'

Selene said comfortably, 'It's never far away.'

'You can't keep it here!'

'You know, dear, you've gone quite coffee-coloured, it makes you look foreign.'

'What I'd like to know is how you got it back!'

'It wouldn't leave me. Did I tell you it saved my life? When I was attacked by two young men – mugged, they call it, don't they? – my fur growled and scared them off.'

'Auntie – '

'I had nothing worth stealing so they were saved from committing a worthless crime. It did them a good turn too, you see. I do think, if crime doesn't pay there's no excuse for it at all.'

Glenda knew she was beaten in the matter of the asking, that kind of innocence was indomitable. But in the matter of the coat she would not be defeated.

'I'm relying on you,' she told the Matron as she left. 'I don't want to see that garment again!'

She took an early train to town next day and shopped for a new winter coat for Selene. She wanted something soft and warm for an elderly lady she told the salesgirl. Had she thought of beaver-lamb said the girl, and was startled when Glenda almost snarled a refusal.

She settled, after careful consideration, on a classic style in a lavender fleck, quite tenderly soft. Picturing it enveloping Selene in a pure and cosy cloud, she carried it away with a happy sense of righting a wrong.

It was not to last. She called at The Harbour on her way from the station to present Selene with her new coat. She couldn't wait to see that little face peeking out of the lavender mist. The colour was so perfect for her. It'll be a real pleasure to see her shrink into that, Glenda thought.

The winter afternoon was dissolving into dark when she turned the car into the drive of the nursing-home. Lights shone from the windows, from the viewing-room came a bluish glow where the senior cits. were watching TV. Selene wouldn't be, television bored her. She would be watching with that private eye of hers.

Glenda's own eye was drawn, after she had switched off her headlamps, to a disturbance in the shrubbery. A laurel bush rocked to and fro, although there was no wind. She peered – the disturbance spread to other bushes. She switched on her headlamps.

Caught in the glare, but not held, on hind legs, forepaws extended, was a sizeable animal. It had a whiteish mask, triangular in shape, like a fox's, and was moving with ponderous grace, dipping, swaying, turning, fur blackish and bristling in the beam of the car headlights.

'Selene!'

Glenda's cry sounded inhuman in her own ears. It was mostly rage, spinning off into fear. She ran to the bushes, ran into them, encountered no obstacle, nothing to stop her, until she found herself at the fence which bounded the garden. She swung round, beating at twigs, scratching her hands. 'Selene!'

There was no-one. Nothing. If there had been, it must have slipped like air through her fingers. Even Selene couldn't do that. Glenda ran to the house, ready to scream at the first person she saw.

It was the Matron, as if she'd been waiting behind the door. 'Oh, Mrs. Lacey, I've been watching for you!'

'It would be better if you watched your patients – and your staff!' cried Glenda. 'Who was it left my great-aunt unattended?'

'There was nothing we could do, nothing anyone could do – '

'Are you saying you can't cope with one frail little old lady?'

'Mrs. Lacey, I've been trying all day to get you on the phone – '

'She's maybe a quarter crazy, but sweet-hearted – '

'I'm so very sorry to have to tell you – '

'You needn't tell me. I just saw her.'

'You saw her?'

Glenda cried, 'Where is she?'

'Upstairs, in her room – '

'Look, I saw her out there in the garden a minute ago, no way could she get back to her room without passing me!'

'Mrs. Lacey, you couldn't – ' The Matron made as if to take Glenda's hand, then clasped herself instead. 'I had hoped to break it to you gently. Of course it's a great shock, it is to us all, coming so suddenly. Your dear aunt passed away in her sleep, in the early hours of this morning.'

'She – what?'

'Died,' said the Matron firmly, to avoid inexactitude. 'We only realised when we couldn't wake her for morning tea.'

'Passed away?' It was a term Glenda derided, but she knew that it was what Selene would do. What she had done. A claw closed over her heart. 'She missed her morning tea?'

'Mrs. Lacey, you couldn't wish her a better ending. It isn't given to all of us to slip our moorings so peacefully.'

'What about the coat?'

'The coat?'

'That goddamned fur!'

The Matron stared wide-eyed at Glenda, her arms tightened about herself, she was seen to be taking a firmer grip. 'The porter burned it.'

'I saw her!' Glenda told Bertram. 'After she'd been dead for hours – '

'They do like you to take a look. Don't let it upset you. She's at rest, poor old sweet – '

'I saw her in the garden as I drove up!'

'My dear girl – '

'It was Selene, she was wearing her fur coat – and dancing!'

Bertram, too, opened his eyes wide, but did not hug himself. He took refuge in reason. 'Darling, it was evening, getting dark – '

'I had the headlamps on!'

'The dusk plays tricks with your eyesight. Shadows,'

Bertram said sturdily, 'do look furry. You've had a shock, but you know it wasn't Great-Aunt you saw.'

Glenda turned to him, she had that inward gaze which he hoped she had lost. 'If it wasn't her, who was it? *What* was it? Fur coats don't dance, do they?'

THE PARADISE GARDEN

SHE WAS GLAD to see that the gates were closed. Last week, thanks to a misprint in the official brochure, she had driven fifty miles only to find it was open day at Parsley Towers and the grounds teeming with people. A wasted journey.

'Tell you what, Joan – ' she often talked to herself, preferred it, she was sure of being understood – 'the weather's on your side. After three days of rain and a warm westerly you'll be able to whistle them out.'

She backed the car into the service entrance, parked it well to one side so as not to cause obstruction and undue attention. It looked, it was meant to, as if someone had just pulled off the road.

There were clumps of sowthistle along the track, a sign of good soil. Dindle or milky dickles were the country names, she had often wondered why. No need to wonder how the plants got here. Each one can produce thousands of seeds to be carried on the wind. Weeds. Someone should dig them out.

The bag which she slung over her shoulder was to all intents – but not to all purposes – a *hand*bag, cream plastic with a fancy snap top, and large, as befitted a woman with a tendency to middle-age. It had, in addition, a false bottom which could be let out to make of it a Gladstone bag, big enough to hold a week-end wardrobe.

Mandragor is one of the great gardens of the South. It has been landscaped to accompany the surrounding countryside, here an orderly assembly of fields, woods and moderate hills, pleasing to the eye and restful to the spirit. The garden exemplifies the control and refinement of Nature. It is designed with precision, shrubs are scrupulously trimmed to knife-edges, borders run ruler-straight from Pole to Pole, the flowerbeds are geometrically confined in lozenges, rectangles, polygons. There are no escapees from among the penstemons, bleeding hearts and Canterbury bells.

She came off the service road to see the garden stretching before her, blocks of carefully graded colour, symmetrical box hedges, tailored acers, pyramidal firs. She said, 'You have to like this sort of thing.' She did, she approved, she found patterns reassuring, there was a beginning and an end to patterns.

She had an hour or so in which to work, although she did not regard what she did as work, it was pleasure, and a lot of fun. 'A little forethought pays,' she said. The last time she was here, earlier in the summer, she had drifted with the crowds, noting and memorising. It was important to know where things were, how long it took to get to and from them, what cover to expect. More by lucky accident than endeavour, she had discovered that the gardeners at Mandragor were in the habit of going to the Rose and Crown for lunch on days when there were no visitors.

Her eye was drawn to a display of Canna lilies in a lead urn. However, they were overlooked, there was a clear view from the house across the cedar-shaded lawn. 'Forget it, Joan, we're not short of lillies.'

A border of Caucasian scabious gave her pause, and next to them pots of the crimson Barberton daisies. She had stooped to explore for side-shoots when she heard the words: 'They come from South Africa, you know. There should be a colour-bar on plants.'

She straightened, turned, saw only a robin eyeing her from the hedge.

'I beg your pardon?'

'Granted.'

'Where are you?'

'You can't see me, not any more. But all of us – English daisies, buttercups, bluebells, Travellers' Joy, meadowsweet, forget-me-nots, willowherb, mallow – you name us, we were here. Once. And we'll be back.'

'Who's that speaking?' She sounded, absurdly, as if she was on the telephone.

The answer came: 'This is Poppy, the wild red one. *Papaver rhoeas* in your botany books.'

She looked all round, near and far, as far as the woods bordering the estate. But the voice was coming from close at hand, from under her feet –

'This used to be a wild garden, don't you know. Me and the yellow toadflax and the blue borage were the glory of it.'

'Are you trying to tell me I'm talking to a *weed*?'

'You're talking to a native, one of the original inhabitants. They came and dug us up. You know what it's like being dragged out by your roots? Of course you don't, you haven't got roots. They chopped down the old orchard, razed our Paradise garden to the ground, brought in cartloads of gravel, put in litterbins and Japanese bridges and staked the place out with a set-square.'

'Where *are* you?'

'It's no use you looking. We were here first and we're buried here.'

'I don't believe this!' She resisted the impulse to part the stems of the Canterbury bells.

'You've gone a funny mushroom colour, you shouldn't stoop, it's bad for the heart.'

'There's nothing wrong with my heart! I'll thank you, whoever – whatever you are – to mind your own business.'

'I'm a survivor, that's what I am. I'll still be here in two-thousand and ninety A.D. You won't.'

Wishing to ignore that remark, and indeed *all* the remarks, she stooped to examine a clump of Rudbeckia.

'What do you want with imports? They won't grow for you, they can't take our weather, they get club-root, rust and blackspot, ball-bud, yellow leaf.'

Something cold, a finger, was moving along her spine. She said sternly, 'I think I may be credited with a sufficient knowledge of plants and their habitats.'

'Tell you what, Joan, you go ahead, dig up as much as you like. Whatever you take will give us wild ones a chance. Our seeds are only waiting for room to come up. Mine can wait a hundred years. I bet you didn't know that.'

'I have no intention of plundering! This garden is a place of beauty and discipline in an undisciplined world. My social conscience would not allow me to detract from any part of it!' She felt better when she had said that.

'Go on, take the Beckia if you like a flower the colour of a hot flush. I warn you, she'll die, she hates being shifted.'

'I'm obliged for the information.' She added, spitefully, that she would welcome any growing hints. In her ears was a noise like the singing in a seashell. She was glad to hear it. It was, it had to be, the source of all this nonsense. Given time, she would be able to explain it. But her time, now, was getting short.

She took out her trowel and separated a piece of the Rudbeckia. As she slipped it into a polythene bag she heard a movement. It was the robin fluttering in the hedge.

The Caucasion scabious and the Barberton daisies could both be lifted and over-wintered in her greenhouse. Working, as was her wont, with a care for the needs and capacity of her own garden, thankfully she felt her alarm subside. She filled her bag, sighing because there was still so much she would love to have. But it would be unwise to give way to greed.

She left the herbaceous borders and turned into an enclosed area which exited into the service road. Here were soldierly ranks of agapanthus and monkshood and a dense white edging of candytuft. Her heels echoed too loudly on the brick herringbone path. She walked on tiptoe. It was as she approached the exit, through a formal Doric arch, that she saw the plant which would be the jewel to crown her visit to Mandragor.

This was a shrub, penicillate in character, with brilliant yellow flowers and fleshy pink seed-pods hanging in pairs like lovebirds. She recognised it at once, the rare and exotic *Pudica florata* from Peru. It is difficult to rear, insists on soil of a special chalky and clayey consistency and cannot tolerate frost. But it is a showy plant, and entertaining. The unripe pods, when squeezed, can be made to explode with sharp reports.

No question, she had to have it. 'Joan, this will make up for everything!'

Her small hand-tools would be useless for getting at the *Pudica*'s root-system. But she had a full-sized garden fork which was collapsible and capable of being secreted in the bottom of her bag.

She had it adjusted and operational in a moment. All she asked was a few moments more before the gardeners turned out of the Rose and Crown. The fork struck something unyielding. When she lifted it, lumps of chalk were impaled on the prongs. She knocked them off and poised the fork for another thrust.

'Better not, Joan.'

She whirled round, but of course there was no-one to be seen.

'Go to hell.'

'That's not nice, I'm trying to help you.' Resisting a more vulgar injunction, she drove the fork into the earth. 'You dig that up and it'll scream.'

'If it does,' she said through her teeth, 'I'll put it on the Esther Rantzen show.'

The fork gripped, she leaned on the handle and the *Pudica* shuddered. She thought she heard a squeak, like the cry of a mouse in a cat's claws. Then the shrub came up, slowly and peacefully. It sank to the ground, lay submissive at her feet. She was pleased to see that it had a good root ball, but worried about the height of the bush. She hadn't stopped to think how she would conceal it. She now saw that she couldn't. She would have to risk carrying it openly to the car.

She shook the loose earth from the roots, kicked over the hole it had left. Dragging the *Pudica*, she turned at the stone arch and looked back.

'You and your scream!' she said.

No way could she get the *Pudica* into the boot of the car. She had to prop it against the back seat, a lanky passenger, with roots on the floor and yellow flowers brushing their pollen on the roof.

Emerging from the service road, she put on speed. When the Rose and Crown came in sight she dared to toy with the notion of going in for a drink. It would be rather fun, standing at the bar with the Mandragor gardeners while the *Pudica* sat in the carpark round the back.

She passed without seeing anyone. In the narrow lanes she drove sensibly, pulling in to allow other cars to pass. It would be foolish to invite even a minor scrape at this juncture.

Reaching the motorway was a victory. It was anonymous, nothing there to connect her with Mandragor. She had every right to be driving along with a few botanical specimens. In company with the motorists displaying stickers to the effect that there was a baby/child/dog on board, she felt a mischievous urge to add the declaration: *Pudica* on board. She chuckled. The way ahead being clear, she put her foot down and was enjoying a modest burst of speed when a police patrol-car shot by, signalling to her to stop.

As she had not even begun to exceed the speed limit, she drove on to the hard shoulder without a qualm. Winding down her window, she saw that the officer was young and personable.

'Oh dear, what *have* I done wrong?'

'There's a peculiar noise coming from your car, madam.'

'Noise?'

'It's stopped now that you're stationary. Have you been driving with the handbrake on?'

'I'd hardly be able to get up much speed if I had.'

'Didn't you hear it? A shrill, piercing noise – almost a scream.'

'A scream?' Her heart turned over. 'I heard nothing!'

'Could it be something you're carrying? An animal?' He leaned into the car. 'What's in the bag?'

'Plants, just a few plants. I assure you, I heard nothing.'

'Don't be alarmed, Madam. It could be some small mechanical fault which can soon be put right, but if not dealt with could be a danger to yourself and other road-users.'

'There is no fault! If there was anything wrong, I'd know.'

'Ladies aren't always the best judges of their vehicles' performance,' he said solemnly, a twinkle in his eye. 'It's an offence to imitate a police siren. Let me take a look round.'

He really was a very personable young man. She lightly touched his arm. 'There's absolutely no need. I'm aware of every sound my car makes. Please do let me off this time!'

'Plants?' He had his head and shoulders inside the car. 'I've seen this gizmo somewhere. Can't remember what it's called.' He seized one of the *Pudica*'s pods and snapped it with a report like a pistol-shot. 'They've got one of these up at Mandragor, the kids had no end of fun with it.'

She said crisply – and she could hardly have felt less crisp – 'May I go now? I have to get these plants to a show and I'm late already.'

'Let's hear you start the engine.'

To her intense relief, it positively purred into life. Gingerly, she depressed the accelerator. Above the muted roar she cried, 'I don't hear anything!'

The officer frowned. 'If you take my advice, Madam, you'll get this car looked at by a competent mechanic. It sounds like something's being ripped apart.'

'Oh I will!' She waved and drew away fast. But as she waited for an opening to get off the hard shoulder, she glanced in the mirror and saw him busily writing in his notebook.

FETCHED

PINTO JONES – CHRISTENED Percy but preferring to be called something trendier – realised that he was being watched. People often looked at him, they looked, looked away, and looked back again. Some stared until he was out of sight.

He knew he was something to look at. He dressed to please himself, took pride in his gear, his black leather waistcoat, sharkskin trousers tucked into cow-puncher boots, brass-studded belt and bicep bangles. He favoured the rooster hair-style, had his head shaved to leave a ridge of hair dyed poster-pink standing stiff as a brush across his skull.

In a month, even maybe in a week, he might start to deteriorate. It was well known that decay set in when you stopped growing, and he had definitely stopped. He had been five feet eleven in his socks since Christmas, it looked like he was never going to make the last inch.

The watcher was an old man, stone-bald, with a skinny neck poking out like a tortoise's. Pinto could smell his general grot from the other side of the bar. There was nothing for Pinto to look at. The bar was empty except for himself and the old man. One of Pinto's tattoos was a dolphin on his forearm. He sat turning his wrist, making the dolphin roll, ready to dive.

'Don't stay long, sonny,' the bartender said. The beer he had drawn for Pinto was half froth. Pinto didn't mind, he disliked the taste of beer but couldn't afford spirits. 'I'm expecting my regulars,' said the bartender, 'and they're particular who they drink with.' Pinto put his lips to the glass and came up with a froth-lined grin.

The fog outside had laid clammy tendrils on his naked chest and caused him to speculate about where he was to spend the night. He had come here to Cornwall because it was supposed to be a place of golden beaches and blue sea. He had expected to kip on warm sands with wavelets and little crabs caressing his toes. All he looked like getting was insults, a glad eye from an old goat, and a cold on his chest. Life, as he had already had cause to note, was great at screwing things up. He felt cheated: someone somewhere owed him something. The fact that he had hitched from London was only half the point. It had cost time, if not money, to come.

'Five minutes,' said the bartender.

'Is there a good hotel hereabouts? With mains plumbing and a baby-watch system?'

'You've got five minutes to drink up and get out.'

'I couldn't settle for less than a four-star.'

The old man laughed. It was the first encouragement Pinto had had.

'This is the Duchy,' said the bartender. 'We want none of your London perversions here.'

Pinto thought of several retorts but decided that a gesture would make them all. He knew when not to push his luck, which was running thin anyway. The barman was brawny and short-tempered, Pinto wasn't in the mood for a fight and couldn't risk damaging his art-work. He put up two fingers and was rewarded by the empurplement of the barman's face.

When he walked out into the mist it was like stepping into cold milk up to his armpits. 'Some corny riviera!' he said aloud.

'You should come in the summer.' He looked round to find that the old man had followed him. Already the damp air was taking the shine off his bald head. 'I'll give you a bed for the night.'

'What?'

'You can bunk down with me.'

'No thanks.'

'On my boat. The Santa Speranza.' The old man giggled. 'Don't let that put you off, she's no saint.'

'I don't like boats.'

'You won't find anywhere else. They're a jealous lot round here, they don't like strangers.'

The mist was not just cold, it was lonely too, you could sit down and die in it. Pinto wasn't used to unhealthy thoughts. He rubbed his arms and watched drops of moisture shaping on the old man's pate.

Down on the beach they came across a little boat with two seats and a pair of oars. 'This it?' said Pinto.

'Give us a hand.'

'Where am I supposed to sleep?'

The old man grinned. 'This is the dinghy to take us out to the Speranza. Help me shove off.'

'I don't like going on the water.'

'It's not far, we'll be there before you can say Jack Kemp.'

'Why should I?'

'It's my name.' Surprisingly strong, he caught Pinto unawares, gave him a shove which landed him on his back in the boat. Next minute they were afloat, the old man working the oars.

It was a question of dignity. Pinto nearly lost his because as he looked up at the old man's gleeful face he felt like a baby kidnapped in its pram.

He managed to struggle upright and sat hugging his knees to keep his feet clear of the water slopping about in the bottom of the boat. Worse was to come. The only way on to the ship was by a rope ladder hung over the side and if it hadn't been for Kemp's grip on the seat of his trousers he would never have got up it.

Nor was there much to impress when he could look round. Mostly ropes and buckets and water-logged tarpaulin. There was a glass-sided hut with a wooden wheel in it, and a yellow old book called LOG, and an array of clay pipes stuck in a corned beef tin. The first thing Kemp did was to light up one of the pipes. Pinto burst out coughing and Kemp threw him a jersey smelling equally of old man and stale fish and told him to cover himself.

Pinto missed his footing on some narrow steps and shot down into a place about the size of a rabbit hutch. There was a table and two bunks, some dirty crockery and a storm lantern swinging from a hook. It moved in slow circles which made Pinto's stomach uneasy.

'How do you want to sleep? Starboard or larboard?'

'Eh?'

'Which side?'

'The side nearest the land.'

'Sit down, make yourself comfortable. I'll brew up.'

Pinto sat gingerly on one of the bunks. He was a tidy person himself, kept his small room in Camden Street bare of all except dire essentials, and only one each of those. His toothbrush and his coffee mug were located over the sink, with plenty of space between them. Asked, which he never had been, he would have said he didn't want to be cluttered. But it went deeper than that: what he wanted was distinction, to stand up and stand out from the crowd, whether the crowd was of people or of things.

Here he found himself obscured by a clutter consisting of anything from garments shaped like old Kemp to a slab of hairy margarine and a gallery of page three pin-ups.

Kemp brought tea, carrying the cups with his thumbs in the tea. 'Care for a doughnut?'

Pinto, being hungry, accepted one. They sat chewing. The old man dunked his doughnut and chumbled it, his jaws revolving as he stared at Pinto with relish of something other than the doughnut.

'Why's it called Santa Speranza?'

'We liked the name.'

'What's it mean?'

Kemp's face quickened, his eye winked, without fun. 'Some Hopes.'

'Look, I'm not staying.'

'You can't go ashore.'

'Why not?'

'You'd never find your way.'

'You're going to take me.'

'Not till after the party.'

'What party?'

'The party tonight.'

'Here?'

'Where else?'

'Who's coming?'

Kemp laid his finger along his nose. All at once he was merry, and Pinto didn't like that either.

'You can't keep me against my will.'

'Stay for the party. I'll take you ashore first thing in the morning.'

Pinto, who was used to looking for where his bread was buttered, thought that the butter this time might turn out a bit rancid, but there was do doubt as to which side it was on. If he stayed, he would get a bed for the night, supper, and some sort of shindig – probably an old folks' reunion, but it would help pass the evening. If he went, he would have just fog and, if he was lucky, a chip butty under a hedge.

'How are people going to get here?'

'Who said anything about people?' Kemp grinned so widely that he disclosed the gap between his top set and his gum.

Pinto's shaven hairs stirred at their roots. 'What's that supposed to mean?'

'She'll come, she's always been one for parties. That's why you're here, I couldn't make her a party on my own.'

'She?'

'My girl. Stella.' Pinto felt minimal relief. So Kemp had a daughter. He had begun to think he was lumbered with a crazy old goat in mid-ocean. 'I don't know what she'll make of you, but you were all there was.'

'Where is she?'

'She won't come till it's all ready.'

'She some sort of mermaid?' Pinto said jokily. 'Going to swim here?'

130

'Mermaid? Grow a fish tail?' Kemp glared, thoroughly alarmed. 'She'd never do that to me!'

'I only asked how's she going to get here.'

'She'll come out of the mist. Suddenly she'll be here on the boat, large as life.'

'Big girl is she? Or on the skinny side? Like father like daughter.'

Kemp giggled, his top plate dangling below his gum. 'Stella's not my daughter, she's my sweetheart. Round as a cherry and soft as a peach. Just what you'd like to find in your bed.'

Pinto wasn't a prude, but Kemp was mucky. 'I'm fussy about what I have in my bed.'

Kemp fished under his jersey and brought out a wallet. From it he took a photograph which he laid on the table. 'That's her, my Stella.'

Pinto hardly glanced at it. 'Where is she now?'

The question seemed to annoy Kemp. 'How do I know? She won't be in hell and she won't be in heaven. She's some place between.'

'Camden Town,' suggested Pinto. It was a feeble effort, but he foresaw a boring evening ahead with Kemp rabbiting about his lady friend who would probably never turn up, and if she did would be an even bigger pain.

'Think she'll fancy me? I didn't have these teeth last time she saw me.' Kemp bared them with pride. 'The last time I saw her she was crossing the bay. She took the Speranza out on the tide and I was too late to stop her. I couldn't believe she was going without me. The Speranza is our boat, hers and mine, we shared the cost, and the work, and we always sailed together. I stood on the jetty and shouted till she was out of sight.' Pinto had started idly spinning the photograph between his finger and thumb. It shot across the table, Kemp caught it and laid it face uppermost between them, with the deliberation of a man playing a winning ace. 'I never saw her again.' Pinto thought he wouldn't blame her for running away, but there must have been an easier way to do it. 'The

Speranza was found drifting and brought back two days later. Stella wasn't on board. No-one was.'

'Did she swim home?'

'From twenty miles out? Ever hear of the Marie Celeste?'

'Who?'

'It was like that. Lights on in the cabin, Stella had made tea and left it. She vanished like a drop of sea water, with not so much as a grain of salt to show where she'd been. Just the cup of cold tea on the table – this same table –' Kemp extended a claw-like hand – 'your same cup.'

Pinto, who had been about to drink, put the cup down and took up the photograph.

Hers was a round basic face, like the faces kids draw on walls: two circles for eyes, two smaller ones for nostrils, and a half-melon grin. She didn't bother with her hair, it was windblown or chewed and stood up in spikes. What looked like a pair of key-rings hung from her ears.

'My lovely girl!' said Kemp.

She wasn't lovely but there was that about her which the photograph couldn't restrain. She had been bursting with life when the picture was taken – and bursting was the word. As she leaned towards the camera her blouse, unbuttoned, showed a good deal more than her neck.

'What makes you think she'll come?'

'It's her birthday, her twenty-first.'

'Look,' said Pinto, 'I'm not being rude, but maybe she went off with a younger guy. You know what women are.'

'Aye, but do *you*? Would you know what to do with a woman if you got one? I tell you, Stella never looked at another man. She only had eyes for me, I was all she wanted. I never failed her – we had some command performances here on the Speranza, I can tell you!' Kemp's twinkle was nothing like stars or kindly lights, it fairly disgusted Pinto. 'No-one to spy, just the two of us at anchor and the sun standing over the mast, or it could be the moon – what did we care?'

The way he was leering, Pinto had no scruples about saying, 'Maybe she'll fancy *me*.'

Kemp rolled up with mirth. 'Think she'd be satisfied with a sprat from the bait bucket when she's been forty years without a man?'

'Forty what?'

'Forty years ago today she sailed away from me.'

Pinto stared. 'And you mean to say you haven't seen her since?'

'Oh, I've seen her – plump and warm and tender – I've seen her every day since.'

'Look, she's got to be sixty-one years old!'

'She'll come back plump and warm and tender, just the way she went, in her dress of watchet-blue.'

'Not unless she's been in the deep freeze. Take a look at yourself and you'll see what I mean. Time doesn't stand still.'

'There isn't any where she is.'

'Any what?'

Kemp managed a snarl before his teeth let down. 'Get off your butt and help me put the flags out.'

So there was Pinto, marooned with a crazy old goat in mid-ocean. He had Pinto tying coloured pennants to every rail and strut and hook on the boat-deck.

'We'll run them up the mast, give her a big welcome.'

'I'm not going up there!'

Kemp giggled. 'Fetch me that line and I'll show you how it's done.'

'No-one can see anything in this fog –'

'She'll have second sight.'

'Look,' said Pinto, 'you've got compasses or something – take me back. I feel queer, I'm not in the mood for a party.'

'We'll soon put that right.' Kemp went to a box alongside the wheelhouse and took out a bottle. 'Come and have a drink.'

It was about the best that could be hoped for, so Pinto followed him down to the cabin. Kemp fetched out glasses and produced a birthday cake. It was surrounded by candles and inscribed 'Happy Birthday, Stella' in white and green

icing. Pinto, who had heard that arsenic was green, determined not to eat any.

'Think she'll like it?' Kemp wasn't really asking because
he was sure she would, just as he was sure she would come,
in a blue dress and earrings that would have taken a bunch
of house-keys, sure she would fancy him, an old man past
his sell-by date.

He poured a generous measure of golden liquid and pushed
it across to Pinto. He drained his glass and immediately
refilled it. Pinto tasted and was transfixed, his throat on fire.
'God, what's this?'

'Best Jamaican. It'll give you a heart of gold.'

'It's burning my lungs – '

'Don't sip like a hen, tip it down!' Kemp took a deep
draught and his jaws shone.

Pinto was beginning to be afraid that craziness might be
catching. He thought, confusedly, if you can't beat them, join
them – the situation he was in he couldn't afford to be left
out. So he emptied his glass. A chariot of fire drove through
his chest and stomach and crashed at the top of his legs.
From somewhere a long way off he heard a shriek. 'Listen – '

'Gulls.' Kemp was trying to strike a match and having
trouble getting the head lined up with the box. It took him
several tries and several matches before he managed to light
the candles on the cake. 'She's got to blow them all out at
one go.'

'Somebody's crying – '

'It won't be her. She never cries.'

'I'm going to look.' But the boat lurched when Pinto stood
up and he was obliged to sit down again.

'Stella wouldn't lower herself to shed tears. She looks
trouble in the eye and laughs.'

'Is that her laughing now?'

'She's not afraid of anything. When the sea gets nasty and
I'd sooner not put out, she says "Come or I'll fetch you."
She's got the heart of a lion.'

'Or a rhinoceros,' muttered Pinto.

Suddenly the candles on the cake started to move. The flames stooped, stood up, laid down flat.

Kemp cried 'She's here!' He clawed his way up the steps to the deck. From somewhere above came a deep mournful moo, causing Pinto's blood to suffer a swift freeze.

Kemp could be heard walking round the deck. The mooing grew louder and nearer, Pinto put his fingers in his ears. When Kemp reappeared he cried, 'She's howling – don't let her in!'

'It's the fog hailer, you fool.'

Kemp dived for the bottle and refilled their glasses. They drank, Pinto to get his circulation back.

The candles on the cake were suddenly snuffed, every one. Kemp chuckled. 'She's having a game with us. Full of fun she is.' He raised his glass. 'Here's looking at you, my darling.'

'The wind blew the candles out!'

'There is no wind.'

Pinto, feeling truculent, rapped on the table. 'Look, there's nobody here but you and me – '

At that moment his coxcomb of hair was rudely and painfully tweaked. His eyes filled with tears.

'Nothing Stella likes better than pulling your leg,' said Kemp.

Pinto clapped his hands to his head. 'Keep her off me!'

'Don't worry, she won't look at you. She's been all this time without a man and she'll have just the one idea.' Kemp's leer would have done credit to the Black Dwarf. 'I've got the same one.'

All at once Pinto, who had had a lot of time for sex, was revolted by the whole concept. He vowed, then and there, to do without it forever, become a celibate. The decision made him feel superhuman, and absolutely pure.

'Just get yourself out of the way when she comes,' said Kemp. Aiming the bottle, he missed his glass and shot the spirit in a lively apron across the table. He mopped at it with the sleeve of his jersey. 'You can bed down on deck in one of the lockers.' He wrung out his sleeve over his glass and got a dribble of dirty brown drops.

'Why should I?'

'Haven't you got any finer feelings? Think we'll want you watching us? When she joins me in my bunk?' Kemp winked both eyes as he emptied his glass.

'You disgust me.' Topheavy but dignified, Pinto stood up and climbed out into the mist.

It was waiting for him, the raw chill brought his tattoos up in goosepimples. The mist was so thick that it was no longer possible to see down to where the water began. He could hear it on the side of the boat, lapping at the boat like an animal. He wished he had kept the jersey Kemp had thrown him and was thinking of overcoming his distaste and going back for it when his bottom was pinched, hard. The grip was like a vice, his leather trousers afforded no protection. Bruised to the bone, he moved fast, not waiting to look round. He ran into a rope stretched across the deck and was nearly garrotted. Someone laughed.

When he got down into the cabin his blood froze again. There was something there, a steady twittering was going on. For a full minute he didn't realise the noise was coming from himself.

Kemp had climbed into his bunk and was lying on his back, the bottle cradled in his arms, out cold. Pinto could have done with another drink to settle his nerves, but he could see that the bottle was empty.

He made a big effort and got himself together. First thing he did was shut and bolt the door to the deck. Then, as he was starving hungry, he cut a wedge out of the cake, hacked off the green icing and ate it. All he had for company was the little blow-hole opening and closing in Kemp's blue lips.

But the food helped. He wrapped himself in a blanket and got into the other bunk. Feeling safe with the door shut, safe enough to say, 'Take it easy, Mrs Jones's boy,' he put up two fingers.

He was awakened by something crawling over his face. It turned out to be an extra large blowfly. He sat up, beating it off. The mist was beginning to let daylight through. His mouth tasted like a pre-war penny. He called out, 'How about some tea?'

The mournful mooing which Kemp said was a fog signal was still sounding outside. Pinto thought the sooner he got back to Camden Street the better.

'Come on, old man,' he said, not too kindly, 'show some action.' He was all set to haul Kemp bodily out of his bunk.

But Kemp wasn't there, only the bottle, snug among the blankets. Pinto looked round, but there was no place else where Kemp could be. It stood to reason he must have gone up on deck. Except that the door at the top of the steps was shut, and still bolted. On the inside.

Pinto's reason wasn't standing up too well. He dragged back the bolt, flung open the door and went on deck. He looked everywhere there was to look, into boxes of old rope, a cupboard full of sea boots and grease drums, a trap door which probably went down into the bottom of the boat and which he didn't investigate because it was padlocked.

He ran round the deck shouting until he looked over the rail and could just make out the shape of the dinghy still tied alongside.

Reason dropped him flat then. He went to the top of the cabin steps and bawled Kemp's name like a baby bawling for its mother. Kemp had to be hiding, under a pillow or down a plughole, trying to frighten him, make him look a fool. He fell down the steps into the cabin, wide-eyed and murderous approached Kemp's bunk.

And saw something he had missed before. On the pillow, coiled like a letter 'S', was a long grey hair, beside it a long black hairpin.

THE DRESS

CONRAD FILBY CONSIDERED himself a confirmed bachelor. It amused him to see the light of battle dawn in women's eyes. Not that he was to be thought of as an object of desire, he preferred to believe that the challenge was one of gender. Women simply could not accept that any man could be self-sufficient and supportive. They thought that, Nature having made the division of the sexes, a woman was essential for the completion of a man. Any man.

Filby had known quite a few women rise to the challenge: married and single, mature professional ladies, academics. A lecturer in medieval French made strenuous efforts to resolve the conflict. He thought she might be inspired by her subject matter which could be coarse, and even lewd. It made him appreciate that totally unlettered child, Daisy Maybrick.

He became aware of Daisy in the basement restaurant of the tower-block where they both worked. She always sat at the same table, eating the same lunch of a sesame roll and two inches of vacuum-wrapped Cheddar. That much he noted in passing – after he had passed her a dozen or more times. He realised her as an entity when she ceased to be in her usual place, noticeable by her absence. He looked for her the next day, and the next, supposed she might have left her job, wondered, idly, where she might have gone.

Then suddenly she was back, her nose pink, paper tissues at the ready. He paused by her table, said 'Glad to see you're getting over it.'

She looked up, blinking rapidly, a habit of hers when startled. 'Over it?'

138

'Your cold.' He nodded kindly and moved on to his own table.

Thereafter they exchanged glances, she in the shyest possible way. He gave her some general consideration while he ate his lunch. She was unlike the other girls in the place, but the difference had to be looked for, at that time nothing about her was noticeable. Mercifully, as he was later to think.

She was small, plumpish and quite comely in her person. Persona however, she did not have. Her hair looked as if it had been trimmed round a basin: she wore, whatever the weather, a raincoat twistily belted at the waist, oatmeal stockings and scuffed courts. Whereas other women made too much of themselves, she made nothing. He found that marginally, at least, the more interesting. Of course she was still a child and there was no knowing how long, or what, it would take to make a woman of her.

She seemed not to have friends or acquaintances. She kept her head down, fiddling with the plastic wrapper on her piece of cheese. She always had, or made, difficulty in getting it off. Filby used to watch while chewing his steak and resolving any points outstanding from the morning's business. He was heir-apparent to the senior partnership of an old-established firm of solicitors with offices on the prestigious third floor of the tower-block.

One day, provoked by her ineptitude, he rose up, went to her table and split the cheese-wrapper with a stroke of his thumb-nail. She thanked him, startled again, and blinking. On her, fluttering eyelashes were in no way flirtatious.

Next day he joined her at her table. The whim to do so came over him as he was carrying his tray from the servery. He asked where she worked and she said 'Rangeroams.' He said, 'The travel-agents?' She was, he gathered a very junior employee. She did not make out travel documents or anything, Mr. Heatherstone did that. She typed envelopes and made tea and went to the Post Office to buy stamps. Her parents were dead, she lived with an aunt in Hackney.

Such was the unpromising encounter which he decided not to repeat. But he had reckoned without Mr. Heatherstone.

The next day her small nose was ruddier than a cherry, her eyelids puffy, she gazed up at him through a mist.

'Not another cold?' he said. She shook her head. It was Mr. Heatherstone, she said, weeping copiously over her sesame roll. Mr. Heatherstone had made a pass. She appeared unaware of the significance of what had happened, knew only that she had not liked it. 'I don't know what he wants!' she cried.

She was not to remain long in ignorance of Heatherstone's wants. He made the proposed sequence clear to her one afternoon. She fought him off. Her face bruised, her lip bitten, she fled down the stairs. Filby, waiting for the lift, moved to check her headlong rush. Beside herself, she beat on his chest with hard little fists. Then relaxed into his arms. Holding her, he found, was a pleasant experience. When, sighing, she drew away, he felt bereft.

The feeling persisted. Sensations he had hardly begun to have, were crammed in those few moments while she was in his arms. He took himself to task, admitted that he was treading in Heatherstone's wake, tried to put her out of his mind. But when days passed and she did not return to her job, she was not just conspicuous by her absence, she was flagrantly missing from his life.

He got her address from the new girl at Rangeroams and went to Hackney. He found her with her aunt, a woman wearing a floral pinafore and curlers in her hair.

Filby and Daisy were married in a registry office. She would have liked a white wedding with bridesmaids. Filby said it would be unsuitable at his age. She did not point out that it would be suitable at hers.

She had so few clothes, and no money. Concerned as to what she was going to wear for the ceremony, he gave her his credit card. 'Get yourself a new dress.' 'A wedding-dress?' 'An outfit. You'll need a coat and shoes and things. Undies.' Smiling, he kissed her. 'Go to a decent dress-shop where they'll find something your style.'

She wouldn't let him see what she had bought. It was unlucky, she said, for the groom to see the bride's dress before they got to the altar. 'There'll be no altar,' he said. She set her lips, she had full rounded lips but she compressed them, into a straight line. It was an indication that she had a will of her own.

Filby was never to forget his first sight of her on their wedding-day. He was hit in the solar plexus. He stared, appalled.

Her dress was not merely unsuitable, it was manifestly ill-advised. For her, and for the occasion. It turned her into a clown: her small breasts moving recklessly in the low-cut bodice, her neck dwarfed by enormous puffed sleeves, her knees – still in oatmeal stockings – sturdy at the opening of the slit skirt. The colour of the dress was vintage claret.

She ran to him, radiant. 'Isn't it beautiful? Isn't it the most beautiful dress you've ever seen?' He saw, with dismay, that she believed it, she could not see what the dress was doing to her. It could not dim her radiance, it burlesqued it. She cried, 'You do like it, don't you? You like my wedding-dress?' What could he say? He said, 'Of course.'

It was the sophistication of the garment which had attracted her, sophistication was a quality she could never have. He felt a wave of pity which was unwelcome, one should not pity one's bride on her wedding-day.

But she was young and unblemished and he was able to excuse her, although she called him Connie, which he could not excuse. One youthful trait he found easy to forgive was her untidiness. It was endearing, exciting even, to come upon a discarded stocking shaped to her young leg, and her bra draped over the towel-rail. Her absurd shower-cap with sponge-rubber flowers only slightly aggrieved him when he found it in the drawer with his clean shirts. He was, after all, twice her age, and prepared to allow the handicap of twenty years less of life and experience. Marrying late, after being single so long, he felt in a position to appreciate the plus and minus of the two states. Asked, he would certainly have recommended the married state. He was not asked, it was obvious that they were happy together.

For the first months of their marriage they did not go

about much. He hoped to educate her to a better dress sense. Although young people nowadays wear most extraordinary garments and combinations of garments, Filby had no intention of seeing his wife a neo-freak.

She took her gentle tuition to heart. She loved him and longed to please, it was not for want of trying that she failed, it was simply her innate disposition to like the wrong clothes, to put on conflicting colours, misjudge the general effect. She even misjudged her own measurements.

There came, as come it must, the occasion of the retirement-party for Linwood, senior partner of Filby's firm – and the public announcement of Filby's accession to the partnership.

Daisy was nervous, it would be her first encounter with Filby's business colleagues. 'Oh Connie, what shall I wear?'

'Don't call me that!' He took her to Harrod's dress department and talked to a saleslady. When he had explained the situation she looked consideringly at Daisy. 'I think something neutral, and we should avoid a fussy outline.'

She chose, with Filby's approval, a corn-coloured silk suit, tailored but softened by the addition of a fringed scarf to be lightly thrown over one shoulder. 'Like this,' the saleslady said, demonstrating to Daisy who had wound it, schoolgirl fashion, round her neck.

'It's not really a party-dress,' she said, setting her lips in that tight little line.

'You look very nice in it,' he said, equally firmly.

The Orchid Suite at Linwood's club was the venue for the occasion. Ladies not normally being admitted to the club premises, the Orchid Suite had its own cloak and powder-rooms. Filby had no sight of Daisy once she had taken off her outdoor coat until she appeared in the vestibule.

It was a repeat of the moment, months previously, in the registry office. He experienced the same jolt, in the same place, where his heart ended and his stomach began, this time followed by a wave, not of pity, but of anger.

She was wearing the claret dress with the over-puffed sleeves and plunging neckline, the skirt gaping open to her stocking-tops. People turned to stare, a woman laughed aloud. Daisy was also wearing her wedding-day smile, shy, tender, blissful.

Anger engulfed him. When she held out her hands he did not take them. 'What the devil's this thing doing here?' For it seemed to him that the dress was there by her invitation. He struck it with knotted fingers. 'Why are you wearing this?' She shrank from him, blinked wide-eyed. 'Why aren't you wearing the dress I chose?'

'I don't like it – I want to look my best for you – this is my wedding-dress – '

'You think I don't know that!'

'Connie, you love my wedding-dress!'

'Love it? I can't stand the sight of it! My God,' he knew his voice was carrying but was unable to care, 'if you could see what a guy you look! People are laughing!'

'Laughing?'

Looking round, she encountered the broad effulgent grin of a young man. Filby cried, 'I can't stand the sight of you in that dress!'

She uttered a sound between a gasp and a sob. She was gone before Filby could bring himself to go after her, those ridiculous sleeves burgeoned into wings as she ran.

She ran into the street, straight into the path of a speeding taxi. Blinded by tears, someone said – tears stood on her cheeks when they took her from under the wheels.

Filby re-married six months later. Some people thought it was out of character, they would have said – and did say – that it should have taken him longer to get over the tragedy of Daisy's death.

Filby himself was unsure of his feelings. He had believed himself confirmed: a confirmed sceptic, a confirmed newspaper-reader, a confirmed wine-drinker, but he was not, it seemed, a confirmed bachelor. The single state oppressed him, he needed another half. He married the lecturer in medieval French.

She was tall and elegant, had impeccable taste in clothes

and wore them with style and flair. She was also much nearer Filby's age. She was not a Catholic and they agreed to have a civil wedding. Linwood was invited to the ceremony, and the Master of her college. Filby was satisfied that it would be a very creditable occasion.

As he stood chatting with Linwood outside the registry office, a woman cried 'Oh, doesn't she look wonderful!'

Filby turned to see his second bride-to-be coming towards him in the claret dress with the big sleeves, the plunge neckline and slashed skirt. It looked like the self-same dress his first bride had worn.

It couldn't be. This, as worn by the lecturer in medieval French, was beautiful.

THE GAME

GREG AND ME have been together all our lives. I do mean
all. Greg's mother took care of me, along with Greg, while
my mother went out to work. We were a month old when
she was wheeling us in a twin baby-buggy. People took us
for twins. We looked alike, bald as coots, pudgy. But we
didn't look alike for long. Greg grew faster than me, filled
out, people said 'Look how that child's filling out'. He was
the up and coming one.

His skin was brown as a nut, I've always been pale. When
we were at school he used to call me Milko. But if anyone
else did, he'd show them his fist – eight years old and he
already had hairs on it.

In those days we played a mucky game with other kids on
a patch of ground that had been allotments. We trampled
down the old marrow-heaps, but potato haulms tripped us
up in midfield. We had no rules, kicked one another when
we couldn't get the ball. Our goal was a tank of dirty water,
when we got anyone to it, we'd duck him. It was just something we did to let off steam.

Then Greg's uncle took Greg and me to Old Trafford to
see Manchester United play Manchester City. We were twelve
years old and that match decided our future. It was an eye-
opener. Greg's eyes opened so wide they stuck out like eggs.
I guess mine did too.

I'd never dreamed there could be art in football. By art I
don't mean paintings and sculpture and stuff like that. I mean
skill, dexterity, talent, cunning. *Professionalism* is what I
mean.

I'd never even seen a pitch like that one. From where we were, way back on the terraces, it was as green and smooth as a billiard-table. I'd never seen so many people in one place. I would have said there weren't that many people in the world. When they shouted all together, out of one throat, even the sea couldn't have made a bigger noise.

As for the game, we saw some of the finest players at the top of their form. I remember a man knocking the ball up in the air with one foot and slamming it into goal with the other before it could return to the ground. Then there was a score by a player running, weaving through defenders with the ball balanced on the top of his head – that's how it seemed, anyway. Stuck on, it looked.

That first encounter with pure football was magic. Greg and me were open-eyed and mouthed. We jumped and yelled with the crowd, though half the time we didn't know why. We were out of our skins with excitement. When I think about that game I can only describe it as a series of lightning chess moves. We didn't know anything about chess either, but we began to see that played properly – ideally – football was an exacting science.

'Did you enjoy it?' Greg's uncle said as we left the ground.

'Yeah,' said Greg. He wouldn't say more. When we were alone and I was rabbiting on about how marvellous it had been, he sang 'Yeah, yeah', and ran round and round me, weaving. We knew what we were going to do. We were going to play football.

We joined the school team, trained willingly – fiercely, you could say. We put in many more hours than the half-hearted school régime demanded. We were sprinting, running long-distance, doing P.T., jogging and juggling the ball every free minute we could get. Like me, Greg had been fascinated by that player who ran with the ball on his head. He was determined to do the same, he never doubted that he'd be a great striker.

Me, I was going to be the greatest all-rounder, the midfield marvel, heading, shooting, dribbling, dodging, attacking, defending – I'd be the best. I knew I had it in me, I'd just been waiting to be shown, and Old Trafford had shown me.

Crazy as we were about the game, we couldn't fail to make progress. We played for school, then, when we were going on fifteen, we got the first invite to play for a local club. They were a mundane lot, twice our age most of them, hitching little games at week-ends when their wives let them off the lead. They probably thought our young blood would liven things up. We thought it was the start of our brilliant career, we put on as much side as if we'd been picked for the World Cup.

We learned a lot playing for that little club. Greg learned so fast he was soon running rings round them. And round me. It was taking me time to adjust to playing against full-grown men. When I saw half a dozen hefties making for me, I tended to get confused and kick the ball out of play.

Of course it wasn't long before Greg's performance was spotted by a scout from the big local club (fourth division, they were), and he went, leaving me with the dads. He didn't want to, it was the first time we'd been split, but football had become our life, the purpose of our life. 'I can't not go,' he said, 'you can see that.' I could, I'd have done the same. 'Put your back into it,' he said, 'and come after me.'

I did. I worked at my game, that was no hardship, I scarcely thought about anything else. And I improved, became quite the little star-turn among the dads. I was pretty nifty at getting the ball away from opponents. If I didn't score myself I always delivered to someone who could. So the day came when I was given a trial for Greg's club and was offered signing-on forms. We were together again.

Not for long. Greg's star was in the ascendant. He signed up with a second division team and it was then I realised that I had never been, and never could be, in the same league as him. We both had this passion for football. His was the conquering hero's, mine was hopeless yearning. I had to face the fact that I'd cut myself out for something I couldn't achieve. It was the bitterest moment of my life.

He continued to spend his spare time with me, couldn't

see it was rubbing me on the raw when he talked about his training and the fixtures that were coming up. When I said wouldn't you rather be with your new mates, what new mates, he said.

We didn't grow apart, we stayed sort of clogged. To me it was the game that counted, and I had lost it. I stopped playing with the club because I'd had only a few first-team outings, spent my time mostly in the reserves. I just told them I was finished. They didn't try to argue me out of it. It's cruel when you say you're through and no-one denies it.

'Get yourself together, you can come back,' was all Greg said, cheerfully.

I couldn't keep away from his matches. I had the dubious pleasure of watching him run round an immaculate pitch, taking the cheers and whistles, embracing his team-mates when he scored, fisting the air or putting his thumbs up to his exultant fans. He didn't know what it did to me.

Once only I saw him fluff a shot, a flagrantly easy one, right at the end of a game. It was all that was required to get the points for his team. He hesitated, swayed, and lost the ball to his marker. The opposition got it away.

'I saw you miss that chance,' I said to him afterwards. 'What happened?'

'Nothing,' he said.

'What came over you?'

He grimaced. 'Nothing came over me.'

When his team was down to play a big away match against a first division team, and would be staying overnight, he asked me to go with him. 'You can put up at the same hotel. My shout,' he said, 'we'll get away for the evening.'

'Won't you be expected to spend it with the team?'

He grinned. 'They won't miss me, they'll be out on the town. It's a temperance hotel.'

I said I didn't want to go. He put his hand on my shoulder. 'Don't let me down, Milko.'

It was surprising, coming from him. Surprised, I agreed to go.

The town was grey stone and Sainsbury modern. The hotel

looked ecclesiastic, stained glass in the windows and an arched oak door. I arrived in the early evening. Greg had gone on ahead with his team. I went up to the room he had booked for me. There were pictures on the wall: one of The Guardsman Who Dropped It, a nice touch of humour, and a big serious technicolour of Adam and Eve being turfed out of Eden.

That was all I had time to see before Greg came. 'Let's get out of here,' he said. He seemed strung-up, irritable. I asked was he worried about the next day's game. 'What else?' he said, glaring. He has a short fuse, so I left it there.

While we were having a meal and a couple of pints at a Berni, he told me he was being hunted by Manchester United. It was a twist of the knife. I said 'What have you got to worry about, for God's sake? I'd give my soul to be in your shoes!'

'You would?'

'You know I would,' I said bitterly.

There was nothing much doing in the town except for a disco which we weren't in the mood for. We could hear a fair going on somewhere, the hurdy-gurdy of the round-abouts and cracks from the rifle-range. We found it on a common outside the town. We shied at coconuts, went on the Dodgems, played skittles, ate candy-floss, and that about exhausted the potential.

Then Greg said he wanted to consult the fortune-teller. He said he was thinking of getting wed and he'd like to know what his chances were. 'Who's the girl?' I said. 'Myra,' he said, 'Myra McCabe.'

The fortune-teller was Madam Sosostris. She called herself a famous clairvoyante. I said, 'She'll tell you a lot of bull.'

She was in a caravan stuck over with magic symbols, eyes and wishbones and black cats. A printed card on the door said it was going to cost two quid for a half-hour's consultation.

She operated with a pack of cards. I was glad there was no crystal ball, I'd have felt like kicking it. She had a hook nose, bangle earrings and a headscarf tied pirate-fashion. She was smoking a cigarillo.

All the old stuff was trotted out. She turned up cards and pretended to get something from them. She was feeling her way, looking for clues. We'd come into money, not a big Pools win, she said, but enough to make us happy. And a highly important change was in store. Greg wanted to know what sort of change. Of circumstance, she said. Greg said would it be for the better. She nodded: we could take that either way. Then she said, 'You're sportsmen,' and it struck me that she wasn't separating us, she was treating us as one person. I thought she can only charge for one consultation. 'There's someone waiting,' she said, 'someone is anxiously waiting for an answer.' Greg leaned forward, asked, 'What will the answer be?' Ash fell from the cigarillo, she stirred it with her finger. 'When the blow falls on one of you,' she said, 'the other must endure it.'

I said, 'What's that supposed to mean?'

She closed her eyes. 'You're examples of a split personality, born apart of different mothers. You belong together in one body, one soul.' When she opened her eyes we were caught like rabbits in her stare. 'I should think that's what it means, wouldn't you?' she said.

Greg was so angry I thought he'd hit her. I hustled him out before he could. 'Split personality my foot!' I said.

He said, 'If the blow falls on one of us, the other must endure it?'

'Psychobabble,' I told him.

Next day, watching the opposing team take the field, I didn't give much for his chances. They were a squad of brick-built men who made Greg look like a reed. I thought he was in for a pasting. I wasn't sorry, I wasn't glad. I didn't care one way or the other.

It turned out to be a game, or rather part of a game I shall never forget. Greg scored after three minutes' play, nicking the ball from under the boot of an opponent and sending a lovely low shot into goal. The others got an equaliser almost at once. Then there was a spell of mobbing and milling in mid-field, attackers and defenders playing pat-ball and no-one getting control. The crowd started a slow cap. One of the opposing mid-fielders broke through and delivered the ball perfectly to their striker. The striker aimed an almighty kick which sent the ball over the bar. From the goal kick Greg roared across, caught the ball on his instep, shifted it on to his toe, ran forward and from thirty-five yards put it straight into the goal. He'd started his victory run to embrace his team-mates when he dropped like a stone. He lay on the grass, arms and legs wide, as if he'd been staked out. We waited for him to get up. He didn't.

I watched them carry him off. By the time I got to the changing-room they were working on him, trying to bring him round. It was no use. They said he must have been dead when he hit the ground.

It was his heart which had let him down. I found out that he'd known it was dodgy, had been warned not to play any more. But his heart was in football, if he couldn't play he didn't want to live. He'd gone to the fortune-teller to ask about his chance of life, not marriage.

I went back to work afterwards, trained all day and every day, except for the day I took off to marry Myra. She spent the honeymoon timing my sprints. 'Hold the watch still, Baby,' I said, 'don't wave it about.' 'Greg used to call me Baby,' she said. 'I wish you wouldn't.'

It was a marvel, people said, the way my game improved. I moved back up from amateur stuff into the football league. I'm in a first division team now, twenty-five out of their forty goals last season were mine. I'm their star striker. I've mastered all Greg's tactics. Manchester United are said to be after me and I'm considering the move.

People say you must miss Greg, you were always so close. It's not like that. I've got myself together, like he said, and he's there with me when I score. We do the victory hug together. My team mates tell each other watch out if you're the first to be grabbed, he'll crack your ribs.

I've got a strong heart, a heart for the game. I'll be playing forever. There's every chance of me getting into the World Cup team next year. Me and Greg.

You Have to Laugh

THE HARRISONS' BUNGALOW was called 'Bideawhile'. Charlie had no intention of biding there any longer than it took him to finish the job he was doing. It was a depressing atmosphere. Harrison, a tiny man, made up for his size with his mouth, started shouting as soon as he set foot in the house. He was some sort of travelling salesman and worked irregular hours. Charlie had to listen to a lot of griping from him. He was constantly bawling Mrs. Harrison out about something she had or hadn't done.

She was no great shakes as a housewife, she left things about, the first day he went, Charlie walked into a washing-up bowl full of potato-peelings behind the bedroom door. She cooked little messes which she offered Charlie and he had to refuse.

His idea came while he was stripping the bedroom wall. It was a boring job, something like three layers of paper to get off. You'd think it was forever, the way they'd put those papers on. That was what gave him the idea.

On the wall he had stripped to bare plaster he wrote: 'Here lies my beloved wife, Rosie. R.I.P.' He often got ideas for a bit of fun. This promised to be one of his best.

When Harrison came home and had finished exercising his vocal chords on his wife, he mounted the stairs to see how Charlie was getting on. 'Taking your time, aren't you?'

'There's a lot of old stuff to come off,' Charlie said. 'Some of this paper goes back a long way.'

'If I didn't have to go to work to earn a living I'd have this finished in a day.'

'That so?' Charlie was careful to sound credulous.

'What's this?' Harrison stared at the wall. 'This writing?'

'I was going to ask you,' said Charlie. ' "Here lies my beloved wife, Rosie. R.I.P." – funny isn't it?'

'Funny?' Harrison rounded on him, his brows gathering, colour running up to his hairline. 'What the hell do you mean by it?'

'Me? You don't think *I* wrote it, do you?'

'It's freshly done!'

'Oh sure, that's how it looks. The paste has kept it fresh, sealed it in.' Charlie thought, if he believes that, he'll believe anything.

'If you didn't do it, who did?'

'Rosie's husband?' suggested Charlie, all innocence.

Harrison turned the meaty shade of uncooked liver. His eyes stood out like organ stops: those words came into Charlie's head, though he was not clear what organ stops looked like.

Harrison went on to the landing and bawled 'Esther!'

'It's nothing to do with her,' Charlie said.

She came up the stairs in a fluster, a corkscrew blonde who would be curvaceous if she gave her mind to it. But she was taken up with trying to keep Harrison's mind off her.

'What the hell's this?' Harrison shoved her in front of the wall. 'Look at this, will you!'

She looked, bending close to read the writing, she touched it with a finger-tip. 'Oh God!'

'This your doing?'

'Of course it isn't,' said Charlie. 'I've just uncovered it from under layers of old paper. You ask me, it's been there years.'

'I'm asking you!' Harrison, squaring up to Charlie, failed to reach Charlie's top shirt-button. 'Who did this?'

'It's someone's idea of a joke. People love playing jokes. You wouldn't believe the sort of things they do. Someone put tomato ketchup in my brilliant white emulsion once. It went such a funny colour, I had to laugh.'

'Another joke like this,' said Harrison with a fox-terrier snarl, 'and you'll laugh the other side of your face.'

'On the other hand,' Charlie said gravely, 'it might not be a joke.'

'What are you getting at?'

'She might be here, this Rosie. If you ask me, this is a cavity wall.' Mrs. Harrison gasped. Charlie winked at her over Harrison's head.

'I'm asking you to get on with the job I'm paying you to do!' Harrison brandished a fist which wasn't much bigger than a ping-pong ball, and hustled Mrs. H. out of the room. Charlie had to smile.

Next day he stripped the rest of the wall, wiped off the inscription and started putting on the paper. Mrs H. brought him one of her cups of tea-cum-coffee. He complimented her on her choice of wall-paper. She said it was her husband's choice.

'Roses are right for a bedroom,' said Charlie.

She gave him a straight look. 'My husband was very upset, he couldn't sleep last night for thinking about that writing on the wall.'

'Someone's idea of a bit of fun, that's all.'

'Your idea, wasn't it?'

'What makes you think that?'

'He was married before,' she said. 'Her name was Rosie.' Charlie stared. 'You've got to be kidding!'

'Why did you think of her?'

'I guess anyone would,' he pointed to the wallpaper, 'with all these roses around.'

' "My beloved wife, Rosie" – why did you write that?'

He started to bluster. 'You trying to make something of it?'

'I just wondered.' She said sadly, 'You see, he was so very fond of her.'

'I'm sorry.' Charlie was genuinely sorry for this second Mrs. Harrison. 'It *was* my idea, I wrote what happened to come into my head. Look, can't we keep it to ourselves? If nothing more's said, he'll forget it sooner.'

'I shan't tell him. If I did, he'd beat you up.'

Charlie grinned. 'Proper little fly-weight, isn't he?'

She seemed as if she might take exception to that. Her mouth hardened then twitched as she looked into Charlie's grin. He said, 'You're better off laughing,' and saw her throat warm up. Her lips parted, she laughed, deliciously: transformed and softened, her face showed what a rarity laughter was with her.

Charlie was agreeably surprised. The signals went off one after the other: red, yellow, green. He was about to step over his paste-bucket and go to her when she said, suddenly serious, 'Rose was such a good cook,' and turned away.

He finished the job on the bedroom without getting another chance to be alone with her. Harrison welshed on the bill, claiming that Charlie had not done the work in the time stipulated, though to Charlie's best knowledge and belief, no time limit had been set.

He soon recovered from his non-experience with Mrs. Harrison, had quite forgotten it. Then his sister, with whom he lived, told him that Rosie had telephoned. He said he didn't know any Rosies, which was true. His sister said, 'Rosie from Bideawhile. You've had so many girls you're bound to forget some of them.'

He figured it out: she wanted to get in touch and was using the name to keep her identity secret. He rang back: 'Charlie here, Charlie Prince I got your message.' Message? she said. 'The message to ring you,' he said. 'When can we meet?' He was mistaken, she said, he was ringing the wrong number. Hearing Harrison's voice in the background, Charlie hung up.

Late that same evening he and three friends were sitting at cards and he held the queen of hearts. His sister came in and plonked something down on the table beside him. 'This must be for you.'

It was a single red rose, long-stemmed and close-furled, a high-class florist's flower.

'Me?' he said.

'You're the one who has dealings with her.'

'Dealings with who?'

'Rosie,' said his sister sharply. 'One of those screwy teen-agers, I suppose. I found this stuck in my milk-jug. How she got in, I don't know.'

Charlie's friends pulled his leg, predictably, about Rosy-posy. He vowed it was a secret admirer of his sister's who had left the flower for her.

When they had all gone, he went out and rang from a call-box. If Harrison answered he wouldn't release the coin to make the connection. But it was her voice, Mrs. H.'s, on the line. She said, straight out, 'Charlie? Is that you?' She hadn't called him by name before, she made it sound private and special, prickles started in his pelvic region. 'Rosie here,' she said, 'Can you come round? I'm alone. All alone. I'll leave the back door ajar. It's Hallowe'en, we'll dress up. It'll be fun, you like a bit of fun, don't you?'

'You bet,' he said.

'Will you come soon?'

'Coming now.'

Exalted, he brushed his teeth, sang as he dabbed after-shave behind his ears, 'Rosie, Rosie, we'll be cosy when we do what we're going to do.' He didn't bother dressing-up, *un*dressing was on his mind.

There were no lights in the windows of Bideawhile. She was waiting for him in the dark. He liked that, it did away with the unbuttoning and unzipping which he found off-putting. He was a romantic.

He knocked over a milk-bottle. It rolled away with what seemed like ever-increasing echoes. When he pushed open the kitchen-door she was there. He felt her presence, warm and spicy, like the smell of a baking cake. All he could see was the little green light on the freezer.

'Rosie?' he said. 'It's me, Charlie. Come out from wherever you are.'

He waited, listening. A tap dripped. She was waiting too. Waiting to be tempted. It was usual, you could say inevitable. However willing a woman was, there had to be a performance, a show of resistance overcome. Charlie understood that it was different for a woman. He too had sensibilities.

He spoke into the dark: 'Trick or treat, isn't that what you're supposed to say on Hallowe'en? What's it to be, Rosie?'

She had come closer, he could hear her heavy breathing, pictured it filling out those neglected curves of hers. 'Esther,' he whispered the name, 'would you rather I called you that?'

He reached out for her, touched only the dark. Her breathing became gusty and uneven. But he couldn't get far on heavy breathing.

'Trick or treat, make it treat, Rosie, I'm not in the mood for tricks.'

The light on the freezer, suddenly intensifying, gave him sight of her. She had bothered – taken pains, obviously – to rig herself out for Hallowe'en. Charlie was of the opinion that she had overdone it. No prospective, or prospecting, lover, should be required to clasp in his arms something which had every appearance of having been a long time dead, even if he could see that it had all been done with cardboard and dirty string. Which Charlie could *not* see.

What he saw was not flesh and it wasn't bone. It was a structure of blackened twigs, like the twigs of a yew tree, with shreds of something connecting where her ribs might be to what should be her neck, but was a twisted rag. Instead of a head she had a sort of cage draped with cobwebs. She had no face as such, yet he knew she was facing him and he wished she wasn't. She had no eyes, but something moved inside the cage.

'Hey,' he said, 'you look terrible!'

He heard a rustle, more of a scratching, really, and realised that the spicy baking smell was gone. Instead there was a bitter whiff which got up his nose. But his stomach gave a final lurch when he saw that she was actually falling apart, dropping to bits as she moved towards him.

Not caring, or daring, to stay and work out how the effect was being achieved, he tried to dodge. He blundered into the kitchen table, sent flying a bowl which smashed resoundingly and spread over the floor some horribly viscous sticky stuff. It turned out to be eggs, but he was not to know at the time.

Trying to keep his feet and his distance, he fell against the cooker, pulling down a pan of cold soup. She came and stood over him, he felt one of the black twigs stirring in his hair.

He lay helpless and in mortal dread. The light, mercifully switched on, showed Harrison in blue pyjamas. At his side, wearing a cute little number in nylon nightdresses, was Mrs. Harrison.

Charlie, wiping his eyes and getting egg on his face, could see nobody – and nothing – else in the kitchen. For which he was profoundly thankful. His stomach struggled back to normal and he struggled to his feet.

Only momentarily lost for words, Harrison roared 'What the hell's going on?'

Charlie said he'd been passing, seen the door open and movements in the dark and had come to investigate. He sounded plausible. When Harrison cried 'Movements? What movements?' Charlie said of course it must have been Mrs. H. in the kitchen.

'My wife,' said Harrison, coming over very quiet, 'has been in bed with me. All evening.' There was a pause, allowing Harrison's temper to peak. 'You son of a bitch, you broke in to see what you could steal!' He advanced on Charlie, his small fists flailing.

Charlie did not move. Somehow he felt he owed it to Harrison to take a pummelling from him.

He got away with a bruised eye and a bloody nose. Harder to take was the old plaster dust in his hair.

I'll Never Know

Recently I heard myself referred to as a 'sensible' woman. I wasn't altogether pleased. The word has tweedy associations. I have never worn coarse-weave and don't intend to start at my time of life, well past what is known as the first flush of youth. And the second and third, come to that. I accept the sentient and rational interpretations of the word, I believe I'm commonsensical enough for most practical purposes. But where does practice end and theory begin? The question has been bothering me since that visit to Araby.

I love all things beautiful, we both do, though Adrian, my husband, hasn't made a study of the beautiful *per se*. I'm known for what could be called a non-oppressive knowledge of antiques. That's to say I don't labour it, I leave people to pick out what they like and can take in from my articles and lectures.

Araby is a mid-eighteenth century country house in deepest Sussex. It's under threat from a proposed new A-road. I had a commission to do a piece about it for the only surviving ladies' weekly which isn't wholly consecrated to Royals, eat-and-grow-thin diets, fashion, hormone therapy and sex.

Adrian drove me down to Araby. He was planning to go and look at a promising stone quarry some twenty miles farther on. He's managing director of a thriving construction business which builds environmentally friendly houses in golfing and pony-club country.

Thinking back, as I do constantly, I can't help putting two and two together and adding it up to an unpleasant and quite unacceptable total. I shall never know if I've got the sum

160

right. He definitely tried to put me off going to Araby. There wasn't a lot to see, he said, Pevsner hadn't mentioned it. I said Pevsner couldn't mention everything and I was actually going to look at the panels.

Adrian said there hadn't been any panels when he was there and I said when was that and he said years ago. I told him these were genuine Rodrigo Clemency carvings which had been boarded over by some Philistine who preferred wall-paper and they had only recently been discovered.

'Come and look,' I said when we stopped at the gates. But he said he'd go to the quarry and be back in time to pick me up about four o'clock.

A woman came out of the lodge house and unlocked the gates. She was big and floppy, held together by something which creaked under the strain. Stays, probably. She told me her name was Iris Woolgar and not to smoke in the house. As she didn't bother to say 'please', I didn't bother to say I don't smoke. We started up the drive which is at least half a mile long and overgrown with thistles and goldenrod. I said it reminded me of *Rebecca*.

The house is the usual Georgian: a portico of three columns with Ionic volutes, sashed windows and the original roof — though there are some ominous holes in it. The front door was a disappointment, it's a Gothic sham with iron studs and gargoyle knocker. Mrs. Woolgar selected an incongruous yale from a bunch of keys and opened the door.

The first thing that struck me was the smell of dust. It was really bitter, bit my olfactory nerves. Mrs. Woolgar obviously hadn't been doing her job, but she probably reasoned that care taken at this point in Araby's history would be a waste of time. I was seized with violent fits of sneezing and she said 'Don't you bring that cold near me,' as if it was a mucky pup I had on a lead.

I said, 'Can you tell me anything about the house?' 'It's coming down,' she said. I said I'd heard it had been a school for girls during the war. She was coming to that, she said, and her stays creaked, I got the impression it was the only sign that her interest was aroused.

It had happened years ago – donkeys' years, she said – and I thought I was going to hear some old tattle about girls being girls. But as it turned out it was quite a little drama which I would be able to slot into my piece, the ladies' weekly readers would just love it.

She said the school had been a 'posh' one, for the daughters of rich people. Discipline was strict, the girls weren't allowed to look sideways even at the gardener who was sixty, or his boy who was, as she put it, 'mental'. So when workmen came to repair the chimneys there was quite a flutter in the dovecote. One of the girls fell in love with a young brickie. As Mrs. Woolgar put it, a bit of hanky-panky went on. The workmen left, the girl was marked down for expulsion.

'Oh dear,' I said. 'Of course it was a disgrace in those days. Now it's a feather in your cap.'

'Hung herself, didn't she,' said Mrs. W. 'In the bicycle-shed.'

I said, thinking I'd definitely make it an apple-tree, so much more romantic, 'What does Pevsner say? A bicycle-shed is a building: a cathedral is a piece of architecture.'

Mrs. Woolgar glared. 'You can't see it now, they pulled it down.'

'Goodness, how sad,' I said. 'Was the girl pretty?'

The corsets crackled. 'Men always think they are at that age.'

I said I needn't keep her, I'd find my own way about.

'Bring the keys to the lodge when you're done,' she said.

I watched her lumber away through the couch-grass and past some mossy statuary.

The house was in a bad state. Winter rains – of many winters – had leaked through to the ceilings: such a pity, lovely old Adamy garlands stained and bloated and some walls actually growing fungus.

Thank heaven the panels, which were downstairs in the dining-hall, hadn't been affected. They were in desperate need of attention, I saw I should have to approach the National Trust, English Heritage, Sotheby's, Christie's and the Antiques Road Show to organise a rescue. Meantime, there they were, those exquisite Clemency carvings, for my delectation and mine alone. I could touch them – I did – was stroking with my fingertips the weird aerial shapes of men and beasts, exploring the exotic flowers, whirling suns and rampant dragons, birds, butterflies, beetles – God, how that man could use a knife! – when a voice said, 'Dirty old things, aren't they?'

I turned round. There was this girl, could have been fourteen, fifteen, sixteen years old, wearing one of those awful gym-slips of shiny blue serge, her hair in pigtails, and pebble glasses.

'Hi,' I said. It's what you have to say to youngsters nowadays.

'Have you really looked?' she said.

I took out a tissue and wiped my fingers. Of course they were grimy, the panelling hadn't been touched for years.

'At that, I mean.' She pointed to the panels.

I looked at her. She was fattish, pale, and had a liberal crop of acne, and more than a hint of Mrs. Woolgar in her. A few years from now I thought, she'll need those corsets.

'It's porn,' she said. 'Know what I mean?'

I said I was afraid I didn't.'

'You can't be that green,' she said, 'at your age. Look.' She moved close to the panels, almost touching them with her nose, she was painfully short-sighted. Where I had been feeling and delighting in sheer beauty, she pressed her thumbs on the wood and squeezed out something quite other. Delicate, yes: fantastical, yes: superbly executed, yes. Beautiful, no. I'm no prude, I just happen to think some things don't belong in public. They should be kept strictly private, part of the rich tapestry of the imagination. Personally I find it too rich.

So there I was, looking at a complex bacchanal of nymphs and satyrs, gods and beasts, and sure as I could be that it had all been innocent and lovely until that girl put her thumb on it.

I got out my little pocket magnifier and took a closer look and frankly I wished I hadn't, it brings out every detail.

'I don't believe it!' I cried.

'Suit yourself,' she said, and she bounced out of the room with a toss of her pigtails.

I was glad to see the back of her, but I was in a quandary about the panels. Should they, *ought* they to be preserved? What for? To deck the walls of some City men's club, or be packed away in the vaults of a museum?

To concentrate my mind I went upstairs, opened doors, looked into room after room. Everywhere was that same bitter dust, undisturbed except in the biggest room of all where soot and old birds' nests had fallen down the chimney.

'This used to be the dormitory.' The girl had got there before me and was looking out of the window.

I was none too pleased. I asked her her name, preparatory to requesting, as nicely as possible, that she leave me to get on with my investigation.

Her name was Marilyn she said. 'Woolgar?' I said. 'No, Monroe,' she said, and giggled.

I was rapidly losing my cool. I started to say I needed to concentrate on what I was doing here.

She said, 'I'm waiting for my boy-friend. He comes every day, can't keep away from me. He's really passionate.' Grinning, she fingered her cheek. 'I gave him a love-bite yesterday.'

I said, 'Does your mother know?' Of course it was stuffy, but I could see that the stage was set for goings-on which I shouldn't care for a daughter of mine, if I'd had one – which thank goodness I haven't – to get involved in.

It seemed to subdue her. She turned back to the window. 'Nothing to see but boring old country!'

I didn't say anything, recognising the young creature's eternal cry of disappointment with life.

I went to examine a graffito on one of the walls. It was of the 'Buddy woz here' type, and when I turned round she had gone again. She had traced something in the dust of the window-pane: a circle with dots and a dash for eyes and mouth. A crude face of the sort not very bright children draw. It was slightly mocking. But what really annoyed me was the fact that her feet, which were a lot bigger than mine, hadn't disturbed the dust, whereas I was leaving size three prints everywhere.

I went back to the dining-hall, determined to be open-minded about the panels. And would you believe it — I didn't — they weren't naughty at all. If evil is in the eyes of the beholder it had certainly gone from mine. I examined every panel, every figure, every bird, beast and flower, took measurements, checked for cracks. Those carvings were quite simply beautiful and fantastical and utterly charming. Nothing more.

I stood and gazed until my eyes misted and the figures seemed to move and I knew it was time to go. Anyway, it was getting on for four o'clock. I looked up and walked down the drive, no backward looks. I hoped I wouldn't see the girl again. Birds were singing, the sun was shining, the boring old country was glowing.

Mrs. W. was waiting for me at the door of the lodge. 'Finished?' she said with her direct charm.

'Thank you, yes,' I said. 'I'll be in touch. By the way, I met your daughter up at the house.'

'I haven't got a daughter,' she said.

'Your niece then. Such a sweet girl, I could see the family likeness.'

'There's no girl.'

'But there is,' I said, 'I saw her, we talked about the school. And other things.'

'Don't you go spreading no nonsense!' She backed into the lodge like a sea-creature retreating into its shell. 'I've got enough trouble as it is.'

The door slammed in my face. I still had the keys of the house in my hand. I pushed them through the letter-box.

As we drove away Adrian asked how I'd got on. Well enough, I said, though there was a girl hanging about — I swear I didn't use the words advisedly, they just happened — she had been a bit of a pest.

Adrian was concentrating on overtaking a petrol tanker. I said 'What were *you* doing at Araby?'

'Doing?' He frowned. 'It must be getting on for fifty years ago when I was there. In those days I was starting out and had to take any sort of job. I went as a builder's labourer.'

I didn't say anything. I put two and two together and snatched them apart again.

When we were speeding along the fast lane he said, still frowning, 'Do you know I believe I've got another of those brown blotches on my face. The wretched things seem to come up overnight.'

I didn't say they're called grave-marks. He still values his looks, so I didn't say anything.